SECRET SOCIETY

ALL WE HAVE IS US

MIASHA

DEDICATION

I dedicate this book to my brothers and sisters— Blair, Quran, Cecil, Tyree, Shamara, Tiara, and Michael.

When it's all said and done, we're all we have.

Love, Miasha

ACKNOWLEDGEMENTS

Thank you, God, for my talent, abilities, opportunities, and ambition. Without any one of these I could be in a whole different place right now.

Rich, you are my heart, Amir and Ace you make it beat. I live for you two. Y'all got me.

Mommy, what can I say...if it weren't for you, I wouldn't be here. I love you unconditionally.

Daddy, you mean the world to me. God knows I am your little girl. If you didn't teach me anything else, you taught me how to hustle. I love you for that.

Aunt Wanda and Uncle Jimmy, you two saved me—well, us. Thank you for everything. I couldn't have done any of what I did without your influence. You two have a special place in my heart.

Aunt Netta, Uncle David, Aunt Merrie, Uncle Blake, Uncle Wayne, Aunt Debbie, Uncle Neil, Dwayne, Aunt Paulette, thank you for being the most supportive family a girl can have. It takes a village, right? Well, thanks for being my village. And to the rest of my family, Robert, Tenika, Danyielle, David, Tiffany, Airis, Terrell, and Ajada, thanks for putting up with my crazy self. To three of the most remarkable women I've ever known, Henrietta Campbell, Coretha Wicks, and Oneida B. Nelson, thank you for teaching me strength and showing me love. I've always looked up to you three and forever will. May you rest in peace.

My siblings, Blair, Quran, Cecil, Tyree, Shamara, Tiara, and even you Michael, I love y'all to death and I want nothing but the best for y'all. Listen, follow your dreams. They do come true. I'm proof of that. We all came from the same place, remember?

My in-laws Pam and PJ, you two are motivating. Thanks for your guidance and your acceptance. I'm proud to call you my family.

My critics and true friends, Rich, Aunt Debbie, Aunt Wanda, Quran, Teren, Kharla, Tenika, and Malikah, thanks for being real and encouraging at the same time. I know that can be hard.

My students Ashley Rodriguez, Marisol Thompson, and Kimberly Smith, you three taught me so much about myself. You inspire me. I write for you. I tell stories for you. I feel for you because it is you I relate to. And let me be the one to tell you, your life is not what was given to you but what you make it. For real.

Karen E. Quinones Miller, you are a blessing. Thank you just for being you, a genuine, thoughtful, and sharing person. I'll never forget the speech you made at my graduation. After all, it was your story that inspired me to actually write my first novel. Not to mention, the extent to which you went to help me get it published. You're something special, you know that?

Daaimah S. Poole, thank you for making yourself available and offering valuable advice. I see a true friendship ahead.

Omar Tyree, thank you for many things, but primarily for opening the door. You've been an inspiration to me from day one, and to have your support means a lot.

Mrs. Ali, it was you who gave me the initial steps to walk up. And look at me, I ran. Thank you.

Teri Woods, Luke and Teri Woods Publishing, thank you for

being the first to say yes. I'll always appreciate this journey that began with you.

Liza Dawson, I'm proud to call you my agent. Thanks for believing in me right away. You could have said I'll call you Monday. But you didn't, and by Monday you called—but only to tell me the results of the auction. How hot is that?

Cherise Davis, I swear you have to be the coolest editor in the history of publishing. I couldn't have asked for anybody more delightful to work with. Thank you for everything.

Thank you to my publicist, Dawn, of Dream Relations. Your timing was perfect. It was God who brought us together, and with a force like that on our side we can't lose.

Algie, thank you for being there once again to help me with some ol' elaborate stuff. Thank you also Ed of Fatboy Media.

Keva, wherever you are in this big and crazy world, thank you for sharing your knowledge and experiences. Be safe out there— you hear me?

Thank you too, Krystal, Cassie, Markus, Global Recording Group, and Deja Vu.

Thank you to all the readers and supporters, booksellers, and book clubs. Thank you to everyone at Simon & Schuster.

And to anyone I could have possibly forgotten, thank you, thank you, thank you.

Ya girl,

Miasha

PREFACE

"You know what, bitch? You fucked with the wrong one! I'm gonna kill you right in front of ya little boyfriend, and then I'm gonna kill him! You played the wrong card this time! You fucked with the wrong one!"

POP! POP!

It still haunts me after five months. I have constant nightmares about it. Sometimes I wish I had died. My life is so messed up now. It's not even worth living. I can't go anywhere. I can't do anything. I just sit here and stare out the window until it gets dark enough to see my reflection in the glass. But then I'm too scared to see my reflection. The doctors took the last bandages off two weeks ago and I haven't looked at my face yet. My psychiatrist, Ms. Carol, was there when they did it. She said I didn't look too bad, but the tears in her eyes told me otherwise.

Ms. Carol was referred to me four months ago. She took a liking to me immediately. Said I was the child she never was able to have. It started out with her visiting me for an hour or two trying to get me to talk about my feelings. Then she started bringing movies, and her visits exceeded two hours. Now she comes by just to keep me company, and no matter how long she stays, I only need to pay for two hours, if she charges me at all.

She's always trying to find ways to make me feel better. She calls like twenty times a day to check on me and she's always so sweet. But truthfully, none of it works. No prescription drugs, no psychiatrists, no funny movies, nothing. The only thing that could make me feel any better is erasing everything from five months ago, from that night.

INTRODUCTION

2001 was a hot year, right after the millennium. It had been a year and a half since I graduated high school and a year since I been workin'—workin' niggas, that is. I was a fresh twenty. Most of my peers were in their second year or so at colleges across the country, and me, I was already in the workforce, making plenty of dough and not needing a degree to do it. School was sickening to me. The whole idea of having to be in a specific place at a specific time at the sound of a bell made me feel like somebody's robot. I wasn't into that shit. Plus, money was always more important than education as far as I was concerned. And when I thought about it, going to school didn't pay your bills but instead it was another damn bill that your ass had to pay. That made no sense at all. So I skipped the college idea and invested my time in other interests.

My friend Tina had introduced me to a lifestyle I would have never deemed possible for me. She taught me something that most chicks already knew. Use what you got to get what you want. The only problem was chicks didn't have shit. They may have had nice bodies or pretty faces, but they didn't have the brains to mentally stimulate the niggas they were goin' after. And if they happened to have all three, they were acidity, snobbish-type broads that niggas couldn't stand to be around. But Tina and me, we had everything a nigga could ask for and extra.

Tina was a chunky brown-skinned girl with big tits and a big ass. She had a real pretty face that was accented by her dark eyebrows, thick dark eyelashes, and dark almond-shaped eyes. She attracted a lot of guys. We always partied together. We frequented all of the clubs and went to every big party in the tristate area, running game on the biggest ballers out there. It was the second Saturday of the new year, the night of the Kickoff, an annual party over in Delaware that was known for being the first party of each year. Tina and me were there, of course, posted up in some fly shit. I had on some army green booty shorts with the matching cropped, open-chest army uniform jacket by Louis Vuitton. I boldly matched my outfit with a pair of vintage-looking cowboy boots in rusted shades of army green and gold. I accessorized with big gold bangles, gold hoop earrings, and three gold chains, the longest one almost reaching my belly button. I had on a pair of gold Chloé sunglasses and I carried an alligator clutch by Carlos Falchi. My hair was pulled back into a neat ponytail. Tina was in some black leather pants and a black leather halter top. She wore a studded belt that rested on her hips, a studded choker, and a pair of black leather Prada pointed-toe boots. She carried a black studded doctor's bag by Marc Jacobs. Her hair was parted in the middle and hung down to her shoulders with a choppy cut on the ends.

"Yo! This party is off the hook!" Tina yelled over the loud music.

"I know," I said. I took another sip on my Malibu pineapple and peered through the crowded dance floor. Lighter and thinner, I was the complete opposite of Tina in terms of complexion and weight, but I was a match in the pretty department. Everywhere I went, guys were like, damn, you gorgeous, you pretty as shit, you're beautiful. It didn't take me long to get used to that kind of attention, and it was only smart to use it to my advantage.

I spotted this dude from across the room. He was hot to death. Dark-skinned with curly black hair that peeked out from under his Lakers hat that matched perfectly with his yellow and purple Lakers jacket with Kobe Bryant's number on it. He had on some hot jewelry too. Tina and I went to clubs so much that we knew just about everybody that came through. But this was the first time I had seen this dude. I was on him. He got up from a table that was crowded with a bunch of other flashy guys and walked over to the other bar in the club.

"Tina, I'm about to go holla at Number Eight."

"I was on 'im too, girl," Tina responded, smiling. I walked around the dance floor to the other side of the club. Number Eight was ordering a drink. There were so many chicks trying to get his attention it was funny. But obviously they were new to it. Guys like him usually didn't crack on girls no matter how cute or slutty they were. You had to swallow your pride and holla at him.

"It's on me," I said as the bartender waited for the dude to pay her for the bottle of Moët.

"Nah, shorty, it's cool," the dude said, smiling and peeling a hundred-dollar bill from a knot of money. He was surprised at my gesture, but I could tell he liked it a lot.

I let him pay for it, which was my plan from gate, but now the air was open for conversation. "That's one of my favorite teams," I said, referring to his jacket.

"Oh, yeah? Mine too," he replied.

"What's your name?" I quizzed as I held my empty cup out for him to pour me some Moët.

He smiled and said, "O."

At that point I didn't know which turned me on more, the

wad of money he pulled from his pocket earlier or the way he licked his lips before he would flash that sexy-ass smile of his.

"I'm Celess," I said, with my hand extended for a formal shake. I was killing dude softly. He didn't know what to do.

"Celess? That's a pretty name and it fits you perfect." He was beginning to flirt.

"I get that a lot," I shot at him.

O just smiled and nodded at my response. He took a swallow of the Moët and gazed into my eyes. He felt me like I felt him, and that was the beginning of a long-term fiasco.

About three weeks later, I met James at the King of Prussia Mall. James was a tall, skinny, light-skinned bull. He played basketball for Temple. He was a hot commodity in the sport. Drafters had their eyes on him.

Me and Tina were shopping when we both noticed James and his friend looking at us in Armani Exchange. Both of them looked good as shit, so neither of us were going to leave disappointed. James's friend approached Tina. His name was Khalil. He was tall and skinny too, but we later learned that he didn't play ball. Instead, he had a variety store that he moved weight out of. James's peoples left him the building and Khalil paid him rent every month. So they both were eatin', but Khalil's plate was just fuller. Khalil and Tina exchanged numbers, and naturally James and I did the same. James was shy and I wasn't in the best mood that day at the mall, so our first encounter wasn't too special. But every one after that was. The one thing that boy could do better than play ball was have sex. I remember the first time we did it. It was a late night in his dorm room. That tiny twin bed was rocking so hard I thought it was gonna break. It was then that I became a believer of that saying, "It's not the size of the boat, but the commotion of the ocean." He almost had me sprung. The only thing that was keeping me tamed was his lack of funds. He would give me a little something anytime I asked, but his pockets weren't deep enough to really set me up.

I met Tariq at Glam two weekends after I met James. Tariq was from New Jersey. He was dressed in slacks and a dress shirt when we met, a grown and sexy type of dude. I was looking fly like I always did in a name-brand something. He offered to buy me a drink. "How old are you, beautiful?" Grown and Sexy asked.

"Twenty-two," I lied. "Where are you from?"

"Philly," I responded. People who weren't from Philly assumed nobody was because they were the only ones who asked where you were from.

"Oh, I'm from Jersey," he volunteered.

"What brought you to Philly..." I motioned for him to tell me his name.

"Tariq, with a *q* at the end," he said. "I heard about this club, and me and my boys wanted to check it out." "What do you do for a living, Tariq?" I got straight to the point. Usually I could tell what a guy did from one look, but he was confusing me.

"I'm a realtor. I own property," he said with confidence as he reached into his pants pocket and pulled out a stack of crisp bills folded neatly together in a silver money clip. He removed a business card that contained all of his contact information from off the top of the bills and handed it to me slowly, making sure I got a glimpse of his cash.

Tariq was something new for me but, hell, he was worth a try. He wasn't drop-dead gorgeous, but he wasn't butt-ugly either. He was definitely different from what I was used to. Tariq was a typical educated businessman. He was always talking to me about investing, buying property, stocks, and all that other "plan for your future" shit. I really wasn't into that, but I pretended to be interested and we wound up having somewhat of a substantial relationship.

The year had begun just right. Exciting and busy. My world

was just beginning. I had three dudes. O was my hustler from Delaware. James was my baller from Philly. Tariq was my businessman from New Jersey. I was up but, I must admit, it was hard trying to juggle three guys. I was playing all types of games trying to keep O from finding out about James and Tariq, and vice versa. Whenever I wanted to spend time with one and not the others I would tell them I had to work. When I think about it now, though, I wasn't really lying. Running game on James, O, and Tariq was a full-time job. But I handled it. Whenever one started questioning me about gifts and money, I'd tell him that I had a good commission month at Neiman's or that I had gotten money wired to me from my mom and dad, who I said moved to Florida. They didn't know that *they* were my good job and wealthy parents. And I made sure to spend a good deal of time with each of them, expressing interest in whatever he may have had going on at the time. Like for James, it was being at his games screaming and hollering, making it known that he was my man and I was there supporting him.

"Go, baby!" I screamed over the roaring crowd.

Me, Tina, and Khalil were at one of James's games at the Liacouras Center. It was doin' it too. It was one of the playoff games, so everybody came out to support. It was all types of girls on James. They saw dollar signs and fame just like I did. But they were mostly college girls from out of town with no sense of style or game. They knew not how to catch the big fish.

"Take it to the hoop, Jay!" Khalil shouted out.

Khalil was hugged up with Tina. They looked cute together, and the diamonds they flaunted helped, from their matching studded earrings down to their his-and- hers Cartier watches.

After the game we met James in the hallway leading to the locker room.

"You did good, baby," I said as I kissed James on his sweaty cheek. He gripped my ass and smiled. "Thanks."

"Yo dog, you on your way," Khalil said, giving James a hand-shake hug that niggas do.

"Yeah, James, you good to be so bony," Tina added. We all just chuckled.

"We gotta go get something to eat. If a skinny nigga like me starvin', I know you must be damn near dead, Tina," James slid in.

"Watch ya mouth, nigga. You play ball, you don't box," Khalil said in Tina's defense.

"Don't worry 'bout it, babe, I can handle his scrawny ass," Tina said.

"Let's go to Friday's," Khalil suggested. "On me," he added.

We walked across the street to the parking lot and played eenie meenie minie mo to determine whether we were going to drive James's Suburban or Khalil's convertible BMW M3. The BMW won, so we did ninety the whole way to T.G.I. Friday's, damn near sliding off of our seats every time we came to a stop.

We all filled a booth at the restaurant. We drank Long Island iced teas, ate Jack Daniel's entrées, and bugged out.

"Tina, you might wanna get you a doggy bag," James came out and said.

"For what? I'm gonna knock this off right here," Tina replied.

"Yeah, but you know you gonna want some more when you get home, you know, for ya midnight snack," James joked.

"I can just take yours 'cause ya bony ass ain't gonna eat it all."

Tina and James was always goin' back and forth bustin' on each other's weight. It was fun chillin' with James and Khalil. They always had me and Tina crackin' up.

Spending time with Tariq was much simpler. He appreciated it when I would show up at his office during the week and treat him to lunch or something. I chose weekdays to be with him because that was when James had classes and basketball practice and O was usually making his runs. Sometimes I would go with

Tariq to show people properties. Not a bad job at all if you like sales. And the commission was heavy. It would be newlyweds buying their first home together or business people relocating from other states or couples with too many kids for the two-bedroom apartment they called home. It was interesting. I learned a lot. I started thinking about buying my own place.

"You really want to do it?" Tariq asked. "Yeah," I said simply.

"All right. I'll take you Monday. You'll be my client." "Sounds good to me," I said, licking my ice cream. Tariq and I were sitting on a bench in Fairmount Park along Kelly Drive, spending some quality time together. He was the romantic type who liked to chill in intimate places.

"What type of house are you looking for?"

"I want a thorough-ass crib," I said, staring into the sunny sky.

Tariq laughed. "You're so hood," he said.

Monday came and I went to Jersey to Tariq's office. He treated me like a client instead of his girl. He showed me a few available houses in Jersey, implying that he wanted me to move out there with him. But that wasn't happenin'. He showed me a few houses around Philly. They were all right but not exactly what I was looking for. It took seven weeks, but I finally found one in Haverford Township right outside of Philly. It was a three-bedroom town house with two and a half baths and a full finished basement. The main floor was newly renovated with recessed lighting throughout, hardwood floors in the living and dining rooms, and a gourmet kitchen with all stainless-steel appliances, granite countertops, and a flat-top stove. It was hot, especially for me, a single twenty-year-old unemployed girl from Master Street.

By that summer I was the shit. I had my own place and I was seen in a variety of hot cars. One week I would pull up to the Julius Irving games on Parkside in Tariq's milky white Jaguar XK8. Tina was in the passenger seat. The next week Tina would be driving Khalil's M3 and I was in the passenger seat. We were the flyest girls out there. Bitches were hatin' like crazy, especially because we were young bucks. And the niggas was on us the minute we showed up at any of the games. Tina was pimpin' hard on dudes, but I was cool with the three I had so I wasn't doin' nothin'.

Tina was messing with Khalil and this other guy named Drake from North Philly. Drake was a crazy dude with more bodies than a city morgue. I begged her to stop messing with him even though he was breakin' her off. So she told him that she was HIV-positive. Tina was stupid like that, but she got rid of him. It was cool, though, because Khalil was really feeling her and he did just about everything for her. She wanted for nothing. I remember days she would call him up out the blue and ask for like three thousand dollars. He would hop in his Beamer and bring it to her, no questions asked. I was impressed and was kind of jealous that James wasn't capable of that, but I let it ride because I knew that once James got drafted I was first in line.

Besides, I wasn't doin' too bad myself, and it showed when my birthday came around at the end of the year. Tariq bought me my own duplex in the Northeast. It already had tenants in it and everything. Typical of him. He was all for black people owning property. And it was a foreclosure so it didn't break him. Plus, he really cared about me and was trying bad to win me over. He was at the point in his life that every man comes to once he's achieved most of his goals and is tired of playing the dating game. He was ready to settle down, and I guess I was the first suitable female to come along at that time.

O bought me a diamond bracelet. He told me he had one more surprise for me. When he pulled up in front of my house in a 2002 Range Rover, I had no clue that *it* was the one more surprise. I almost fainted, but I didn't let him see that. He was the type of dude that had to believe you was used to getting shit like a $80,000 car for a birthday gift after only one year of knowing a nigga. So I kept my cool. Besides, I wasn't a fool. Niggas who bought their girls cars were smart. They knew they could take it back in a heartbeat the first minute she started trippin'. Needless to say, I kept my shoelaces tied tight.

James somehow scraped together some money and took me to Jamaica for a week. It was like a double date. Khalil took Tina. We had a ball. James and Khalil were straight-up hood niggas, which meant you could go anywhere in the world with them and have fun. They knew how to make the best of any situation. Being in the islands helped too, but they made the trip. When they weren't busting on people, they were taking us on crazy shit. We did everything from Jet Skied to scuba dived. We even panhandled just to fuck with people. We would have skydived if it weren't for Khalil being afraid of heights. It was a week well spent, and even though it didn't cost nowhere near my other gifts, it was the most memorable. I couldn't imagine spending a week in Jamaica with Tariq or O, anyway. Tariq would have probably spent the whole time buying time-share and O probably would have wound up finding a weed connect and setting up shop. So, even though the trip exposed how broke James was compared to O and Tariq, I was glad he was the one I spent it with.

I was on cloud nine. Nothing made me happier than great sex and money, and that's what O, James, and Tariq were good for. With the three of them, I was having shit my way, and playing the game was giving me more and more of a rush. I couldn't wait to see what the new year had in store for me. Or maybe I could.

JANUARY

In 2002, Tina and me brought the New Year in together like always. But instead of club and barhoppin' in Philly, we went to Vegas to hook up with these white guys named Terry and Derrek from L.A. They were some rich-ass investors who Tina met at a Sixers game last season. Khalil got locked up for drug trafficking right around Christmas, shortly after we got back from Jamaica, so she was interested in broadening her horizons. She came to the realization that the type of guys she was used to dealing with would only end up where Khalil was, or dead, and she needed stability. Terry and Derrek were twins. They looked all right, but they were old and it showed. Derrek was for Tina. He was short, buff, and bald. I called him Mr. Clean behind his back. My dude Terry was similar to Derrek in height, but he was less buff and more flabby, and he was only bald in the middle. Both of them dressed very well, in Italian-made suits, expensive jewelry, and silk and cashmere shit, which compensated for what they lacked in the physical department.

We met up with Terry and Derrek at the MGM Grand Hotel on the strip. They already had a room for us. It was a huge two-bedroom suite on the top floor. Our view was off the hook. We could see the whole strip and at night—it was a sight to see. So many bright lights, fancy cars, and people. Guys and girls filled the streets, walking, driving, or posted up on the strip. It was exciting. Every bone in my body anticipated action. Tina and me were turning so many heads, and if we were selfish and careless bitches we could have jumped in one of them Ferraris quick, right in front of Terry and Derrek. But that wasn't our steez. And besides, Terry and Derrek gave us no reasons to. They were both filthy rich and had no problem peelin' off. We were like their trophies, and they kept us polished and lookin' good. We drank, partied, and fucked a lot, and we even did some shopping at the Venetian. It was fun as hell out there, but when the week was up I was ready to go home. I missed my house. That is, until I got there.

The first thing I noticed when I walked through my front door was the blinking on my answering machine. I checked the caller ID first and saw that James had called me about a thousand times. I told all my dudes that I was going to Vegas with Tina for a few days, so I didn't know why James blew up my phone. Besides, he was in Houston negotiating a contract with the Rockets. What would he be all pressed to get in touch with me for? I thought.

Most of the messages were short. "Babe, it's me, holla back," "Babe, pick up the phone," "Celess, where you at," etc., etc., etc. But the last one was long and detailed.

"Celess, what's up with you? I heard some wild stuff about you. You need to call me as soon as possible, because if what I found out is true you're goin' to have some serious problems."

I called James back on his cell. He answered on the first ring.

"Yo, what's up?" he whined. "Hey, baby," I said. "What's up?" "You didn't get my message?"

"Yeah, what's up, what hater told you somethin'?" I asked, trying to convince him that it was a lie before even knowing what the hell he was going to tell me. "Yo, I'm at an NBA party, right, and these broads come over and try to holla at me and this other bull. So the one broad had a fuckin' Adam's apple and shit, right? So the bull I was with cursed the broads out. Then he started tellin' me about these two joons from Philly who be playin' dudes the same way. They dress and live like women, but they really men."

I would have liked to have passed out. Fuck! I thought. I was already trying to work up a plan. But before I went jumping to conclusions, I waited for James to finish.

"Then dude said yall names, Tina and Ce-fuckin'-less. Yo, say it ain't so, Celess," James pleaded.

"What?" I yelled. "A man? That is some insane shit, James. I can't believe you're bringing me this high drama!" I was trying to play it off. I didn't know what else to do.

"But yo right, I started thinking," James said, "and we never fucked in the light. And you always make me hit it from the back. What? I be puttin' it in ya ass? And yo, you ain't never ask me to eat you out or nothin'."

"If I remember correctly, you told me you didn't eat pussy!" I shot back at him.

"Yeah, but I tell every joon that and it don't keep them from asking me to make an exception. Just tell me what the fuck is goin' on, please."

James sounded like he was going to cry. I was actually starting to feel bad. I never thought I would have to come clean to anybody before. I thought it would either come down to them finding out during sex and liking it so much that they wouldn't care, or I would stop dealing with them before they could ever figure it out. Tina didn't school me to this part of the game. I didn't know whether to continue denying it or just apologize and beg for his forgiveness. I knew that I would not be able to get away with denying it because as soon as he came back to Philly he would be checking for a penis. So I decided to just tell him the truth. "Look, James, I'm sorry," I started out, then I immediately started crying.

"You bitch! You fuckin' dirty bitch! How the fuck could you do this shit to me, Celess? Is ya fuckin' name even Celess?"

"James, I'm so sorry. I knew you wouldn't have got with me if you knew, and I was feeling you," I whined. "Bitch, is you crazy? You damn right I wouldn't have got with you! You a fuckin' man! I'm not fuckin' gay! You's a crazy bitch! You know what yo, don't fuckin' call me! If you see me anywhere, don't fuckin' say shit to me! If you even fuckin' look my way I will fuckin' hurt you! I swear to God!"

Click.

I held the phone to my ear even after James had hung up. I listened to the dial tone while I cried and felt sorry for myself. I knew I should not have done that to James and he was the one who deserved sympathy, but this made me realize that I would never sincerely get what I wanted. I would never be a woman, no matter how dressed up I got or how much makeup I wore or how many hormones I took.

I needed to get out of the house. I needed a drink.

I called Tina.

"What? Well, who the fuck told him that? Who in the NBA found out about us?" Tina asked.

We were in her black-on-black GS 400, a gift from her white friend Derrek, on our way to Main Street in Manayunk.

"I don't know. I didn't ask him all that," I said, still crying.

"Girl, wipe your eyes. Don't be crying over no man.

Shit, James was the brokest of the three, anyway," she said frankly.

"That's not the point, though, Tina," I explained. "I really hurt him. He sounded like he was going to cry." "Well, you know what, they do it to women all the time, play with their hearts. He'll get over it." "But what you gonna do about Khalil?" "What about Khalil?"

"You know James is gonna tell him, if he didn't already," I explained.

"Khalil is doin' time. James ain't gonna be in touch with him for a minute. Especially with James going to the NBA, him and Khalil will probably lose touch."

Tina had all the answers, but she didn't understand. Yeah, she'd been dressing up since she was fourteen, but she never been in my or James's situation before. She never even came close to a guy finding out about her. Hell, when I met her I thought she was a girl. It was ninth grade. We had a class together. She was dressed so fly. I admired her. I was still playing a straight role to a certain extent. I dressed like a regular guy. I acted like a regular guy. But I wasn't a regular guy on the inside and Tina could sense that. When she told me she was a dude, I flipped out. I didn't believe her. It came down to her showing me her dick. It wasn't on some gay shit either, because I was not at all attracted to her. She was too pretty and looked too much like a girl. I wanted to do the same thing she was doing. I wanted to live my life as a girl. I figured it would be much easier on me messing with guys as a girl than as a guy. But now I didn't know what to think. I felt fucked up.

I got drunk as shit off of apple martinis. Tina dropped me off home at about eleven o'clock. I went right to sleep.

Ding-dong. Ding-dong. Ding-dong. I jumped up out of my sleep. The clock said twelve-fifteen. I was fucked up. I managed to get out of bed and go see who was at my door. I could see through the peephole that it was Tariq. He was dressed casual in a leather jacket, a baseball cap, a white T-shirt, and some baggy jeans. Then I remembered he took off from work to spend the day with me. I didn't open the door. I ran into the bathroom and tried to get myself together. I couldn't let him see me like that. I was a mess. He kept ringing my bell. Then he started ringing my phone. I answered.

"Hello," I said, sounding sleepy.

"Wake up, sleepyhead, I'm outside your house," he said.

"Oh, shit, Tariq, I forgot all about our plans," I confessed.

"Well, now that your memory is refreshed, can you come open the door?"

"Yeah, hold up a second."

I put myself together somewhat and let Tariq in. "Who did you go out with last night?"

"Tina got me drunk as shit." I switched the blame.

"I see," he said.

"Give me a minute to do something with myself and we can go out," I said.

"Just get in the shower," he said. "We can chill here, watch movies, and order in," he suggested.

That was a bet. I turned on the faucet so I could take a long bath. But I made sure to lock my bathroom door. Good thing too, because Tariq did try to come in. I did all of the important things in the bathroom, like tape up my thing and put on my bra and panties. I slipped into some J Lo sweats and some slippers. I brushed my hair back into a ponytail and bobby-pinned the weave onto it. I put on a little makeup and joined Tariq in the family room.

Tariq had already made himself comfortable. He had taken his jacket and shoes off and was surfing through the channels. I felt a lot better after that bath. I just needed to get some food. We ordered Chinese and pigged out for the day. It was relaxing.

When Tariq left at seven o'clock I began to feel bad all over again. I started feeling bad for James. Tariq and O too—I just kept thinking what would happen if they found out. I never used to worry about this, but since James found out, I realized that it was possible. As usual, I called Tina.

"Tina, what you doin'?"

"You mean *who* I'm doin'," she joked.

"No, I meant *what* like I said," I joked back. "I'm working out," she said.

"How did we get into this, Tina?"

Tina knew what I was getting at. "Why are you still trippin' over dude?"

"I don't know. I'm nervous that they might all find out. And what if James come back to Philly trippin' out on me?" I worried.

"James isn't the type. Plus he got a rep to think about too. You think he want people to find out that he fucked a man? He won't say or do shit, trust. You just need to replace him and move on," Tina demanded.

She had a point. James was probably busy trying to get this whole thing out of his head.

"You're right," I said.

"Matter of fact, we're going to Delaware tonight," Tina said.

"For what?"

"It's the Kickoff tonight, the first party of the year. We haven't missed it in two years, so let's not start now. Plus, I'm sure we'll see some new faces. Some fine-ass ones that will get your mind off James."

"All right," I agreed. "I need to get back in the swing of things, anyway."

I had on a short blue Dior skirt with the matching signature Dior leg warmers, a white fitted blouse, and my blue mink. I looked fly. Tina rocked her waist-length black mink with a short black cutout dress. She had on stiletto pumps and nude stockings. She looked tight too. When we walked in the club, everybody stopped and stared, including O, who hadn't even called me to tell me he was back in town.

"The last I checked you was in Baltimore handling business," I said with sass.

"And wasn't you in Vegas?" he asked.

"You knew I was only staying in Vegas for a couple of days, but I had no idea when you were supposed to come back. I relied on a phone call."

"My bad, baby," O said as he grabbed my waist. O didn't seem like himself. I could tell he was high, but it was something else about him that didn't sit right with me. He kissed me on my cheek and then let go of my waist. He told me to go to the bar and order Tina and me a drink on him, then he disappeared in the crowd.

"A Smirnoff Ice with raspberry, please, and an apple martini," I yelled to the bartender.

I took a seat on the stool next to Tina.

"I can't believe that nigga didn't call me when he got back," I told Tina.

"Don't sweat it, he look damn good," Tina said.

O did look good that night. He had on jeans, a white T, his camel-colored mink, and some fresh tan Tims. Then he topped it off with yellow diamonds that sat in his gold chain and earrings and a gold-face Jacob on his wrist. He was definitely a stunner.

I took a sip of the Smirnoff and chilled. I couldn't work my magic on nobody because O was there. Tina started talking to some suave-ass dude with some leather pants on. I ordered a second Smirnoff and started feeling a little buzz. I was sitting at the bar, feeling the music and just chillin', when something caught my eye.

O was taking pictures with some broad on his lap. And this girl was kissing all on his neck. He was just smiling and being real disrespectful. I tapped Tina on her shoulder.

"This nigga is tryna play me," I said with an attitude.

Tina looked in the direction of my eyes and saw O acting a fool. She snapped as if he was her man instead of mine.

"Oh, hell, no, go over there and check that nigga and that bitch!"

"He knows I'm the fuck here. Why would he do some stupid shit like that?"

Tina hopped off the stool and grabbed my hand. "Come on. This nigga playin' his self," she said as she led me through the crowd.

"What the fuck is the deal?" Tina snapped at O. O had a confused look on his face. I guess he was wondering why Tina came at him like she did when he wasn't her man.

I stepped in. "O, can I holla at you for a minute?"

O got up from the chair and moved the girl to the side.

"What's wrong, baby?" the girl asked.

"Nothin', just give me a minute," O responded. I was pissed off.

"What's up?" O asked as he walked toward me.

He put his arm around my waist and slowly walked me a few steps away from the girl and Tina. I had a blank look on my face and was speechless at first. I was about to flip out on that nigga, but I told myself to be easy.

"O, please don't act like you wasn't just disrespectin' me. Don't get me wrong, I'm not the jealous type, but damn, all that was unnecessary. You can do whatever you want on your own time, but when I'm in your presence, you're on my time. You feel me?"

O put on that confused face again. "What are you talking about, baby?" he asked.

His eyes were glassy. He seemed real disoriented. He was pissing me off even more by acting nonchalant. "Is everything okay?" the girl came behind O and asked.

Tina followed her and responded for O. "Everything is just fine," Tina said.

The girl rolled her eyes. "O, is everything okay?" she asked, placing emphasis on his name.

"Bitch, I said everything is fine. O is talking to his girl right now!" Tina yelled.

"I'll show you a bitch, bitch!" the girl shot back, walking over to Tina.

O was still acting nonchalant like everything was everything. But I wasn't about to let Tina embarrass herself for no cheap-ass whore. I stood in front of Tina and started pushing her out of the club. Meanwhile, O disappeared again and the girl was steady screaming shit. You fat bitch this, you fat bitch that. And Tina was screaming back, "I got more money than ya bum ass!" That night was crazy.

"Celess I'm sorry. I was feelin' it," O tried to explain. "Well, you need to leave whatever that shit was alone, 'cause it had you lookin' slow and shit."

"Yeah, that E will do that to you. You forgive me, sweetheart?"

"You owe me for this one," I said.

"Come through and I'll make it up to you."

It had been a week since the incident at the club, and this was the first time I was hearing from O. He was about to be cashed in. I was losing love for him. He had me at my point where I was ready to juice him dry and then cut him off. I had suspected he put another girl in my place and bumped me to number two or something. I couldn't understand why he was frontin' on me like that, but it was really making me not care anymore.

I told O I would come through, but instead, I went to get my hair done. The shop was empty, being as it was a Tuesday afternoon. My bull Steve did my hair for me. And when Steve did my hair it was an all-day affair because he would spend more time gossiping than actually doing my hair.

"Those shoes are cute," Steve commented on my Chanel boots.

"You like 'em?" I asked for no reason at all.

"Yeah, they hot. My girl would look good in them." Steve was an ITCH—an in the closet homo. He always talked about a girl who nobody ever seen. But that particular afternoon he indirectly came out. "Yo, how do you do it?" he whispered. "What?" I asked.

"Walk in those heels."

I thought Steve was going to ask how I got away with being a woman. I was sure he knew. But maybe he didn't.

"I'm used to it," I said.

"This guy I know, he's gay and he's gonna start dressing up like a chick and get a sex change, the whole nine, but he said he don't know how the hell he gonna walk in heels," Steve said, laughing.

Bingo, I thought. Steve had to be gay. Anytime a man uses the word *gay* instead of *faggot* to describe a gay man, that's a sign that he himself is gay. Besides, he did hair. Damn, it's a lot of us out here, I thought. But I didn't say anything. I just listened to Steve tell all his business and everybody else's business.

Ring! Ring!

"Hello," I answered my cell phone. "Where the hell you at?" O asked. "I just left the hairdresser," I said.

"You a nut for telling me you was coming down here," he said. "I might as well go shoot dice," he continued.

I knew what that meant. He had money to spend, and I didn't want to miss out on that.

"I'm on my way, damn, can I get cute first?" I whined.

"You could have called a nigga."

"My bad. I'll be there in like a half," I said.

I pulled up to O's house twenty minutes later. Ninety-five was empty. As soon as I walked in, he grabbed me and started kissing me. He started stripping me. I stopped him from removing important articles of clothing, but he was persistent.

"Who you been giving my pussy to?" "Nobody," I said, trying

to control his hands. "Then why you haven't been giving it to me?"

"Boy, you been trippin' since you got back from Baltimore. What were they feedin' you down there?"

"It's not what they been feedin' me, it's what they haven't been feedin' me. I'm lacking pussy. Can you feed me some pussy?"

I grabbed his hand just in time to stop him from grabbing my balls. O never acted like this before. Usually I took charge and he just followed my lead. What the hell he was doing I didn't know, but it was bound to get me killed. I had to think of something quick.

"My period is on," I blurted out. O stopped kissing me.

"Damn!" he said. "Thanks for blowin' my high."

He sat down on the couch and patted his dick as if he was trying to calm it down. I sat down next to him, trying to keep a distance. He grabbed my hand and put it on his penis.

"Pull it out," he said.

I did. I stroked it for him. He started getting into it, and he grabbed my head and forced it down on his dick. I sucked it. What the hell, I figured I owed him that much for not having a pussy he could eat.

I left O's house with $500. This was the icing on the cake. I knew for sure he had somebody else. Five hundred dollars meant he was giving half of my money to another girl. I was pissed about it but I let it slide. He obviously had his reasons for playing me. I went home and called it a day. I put on Two Can Play That Game and fell back.

FEBRUARY

I evaluated my situation. I had lost James and I was in the process of losing O. Tariq was the only one I had a grip on. Tariq was still paying my mortgage, but I needed another James to pay my other bills. O was still lookin' out on my wardrobe and pocket money, but it was nowhere near what I used to get from him. I needed to make a comeback. Tina was getting bored too. White Derrek would wire her money ever' so often and this Puerto Rican hustler named Jahuan from down the badlands was taking her out and would buy her some shoes here and there, but that wasn't enough. We took a trip up New York to go to a fight and met some guys just in time for Valentine's Day. Tina put me down with boxers. She used to mess with one back before her and I met, and she told me all about the kind of money some of them make.

The fight was interesting. I'd never been to a live boxing match before then. We went to the after-party at the Pierre on Fifth Avenuc, which was where the meeting and greeting began. This brown-skinned bony dude came over to Tina and me and told us that his friend wanted to holla. We were prepared to tell bull to get lost, but when we saw that his friend was Christopher Talley, the super middleweight champion of the world, we were like all right.

"What are yall drinking?" Chris asked. "Apple martini." It was Tina's favorite drink. "A peach schnapps," I said.

"Good fight," Tina said. "Thank you," he replied.

Chris looked like he could have been cute if it wasn't for the missing teeth and permanent scars that came with boxing. But he was dressed nice, and it was obvious he had money. Tina wound up with him, and I settled for another fighter, Shawn, who was from the same camp as Chris. We all ate and drank and then headed up to a hotel room. After I went down on Shawn and Tina did God knows what with Chris, we all exchanged numbers and started dealing with each other regular. I even spent Valentine's Day with Shawn at his house in Brooklyn. That pissed O off.

"How the fuck you goin' spend Valentine's Day with some other nigga?" O screamed in the phone.

"When you decided to have somethin' on the side," I responded.

"So, you fuckin' this nigga?" O asked, as if I had already admitted it to him.

"Don't act like you don't know what I'm into," I said, being real for the first time in our so-called relationship.

I was tired of O's recent bullshit. We both had ulterior motives, shit.

"Fuck you, bitch!" he said right before he banged on me.

I wasn't mad, though. Actually, I couldn't have cared less. Shit, it was time for O to take what he dished. I was moving on. And I guess that's exactly what it took to bring O back to reality, because his ass started paying me a lot more attention after he found out I was messin' with somebody else. He called me more and wanted more of my time. I gave it to him only because he was closer and more convenient than Shawn, who traveled a lot.

Meanwhile, Tina and I were making all kinds of plans for All-Star weekend. It was so convenient that it was in Philly that year. We went down South Street and had some things made. I ordered a baby pink leather suit with white stripes going down the side of the legs and arms like the Adidas sweat suits. The shirt hung off the shoulders. It was hot. I bought a baby pink Kangol to go with it. Tina ordered the Iverson jersey with the red leather sleeves and the red leather ties on the sides. It was hot too. She paid $349 for that shirt. She bought some Frankie B. jeans from down Charlie's in Old City and some hot red Miu Miu boots to go with it. That was just for the game, though. We still had to buy outfits for the other parties. I bought a J Lo jeans outfit that had tan ties up the legs and the jacket. Bought tan Chanel boots, a tan knitted Chanel bag, and a tan knitted Chanel hat to match. Hats and things that tied up were hot shit that year. Tina did a winter white leather Dolce & Gabbana miniskirt, a winter white boat-neck sweater, and some winter white D&G knee boots.

The Friday before the game we went to an invite-only in Atlantic City. There were a lot of upscale people there and a few losers who probably worked in the mail room and got the hookup on some invitations. Tina and I almost fainted when we saw Morris Chestnut sitting in a booth. We kept our cool, though. We basically spent that night drinking and mingling. This guy approached me while Tina was dancing with somebody.

"You are beautiful," he said. "Thank you," I responded.

I was trying to be nice even though I already knew I wouldn't have given him the time of day. He was so corny it was sad. He had on some slacks and a dress shirt. The top button of his shirt was open, revealing a gold herringbone chain. He was wearing what looked like a high school class ring on his pinky finger. And to top things off he had a part in the middle of his low haircut.

"What's your name?" he asked. "Celess," I answered.

I decided to play with dude a little before taking the knife to his throat.

"What's yours?" I asked. "Jared," he replied.

"What do you do, Jared?"

"I play the flute. What about you?" "I play men," I said firmly. He just grinned.

"Well, it was nice meeting you," he said, and walked away.

I figured he would do that. Tina came over to me just in time for me to tell her about the clown who had just approached me, but she beat me to the punch.

"How about I'm dancing with the bull, giving him the butt and everything. So we talking and I'm probing him. I asked him what kind of car did he drive. He talking about a Cavalier with twenties and an Alpine stereo—"

"A souped-up Chevy," I butted in.

"Basically," Tina continued. "Then I asked him if he had a house. He talking about he's the man of the house. Guess who the women of the house were!"

"His wife and daughter?" I asked, playing the guessing game with her.

"No! His mom and his grandmom!" Tina said, bursting out into laughter.

"Well, dude I was just talking to plays the flute," I said.

"Get the fuck outta here," she said, still laughing.

We figured we would have better luck meeting some real niggas at the All-Star game.

The First Union Center was packed. The parking lots all looked full. Thank God Tina and me rented a stretch Hummer. If we would have drove we would have spent the whole game looking for parking. When we pulled up to the entrance and stepped out the car, all eyes were on us. Bitches were waiting to see some niggas hop out behind us, and when that didn't happen, they were hatin'. It was written all over their faces. They probably were thinkin', How them bitches get that by themselves? Inside, the halls were crowded. People were making their way to their seats. The concession lines were long, and of course posted along the walls were lines of guys and girls, all dressed in their flyest shit. There were furs, diamonds, and designer labels galore. "Pink Sweat Suit," a familiar voice called out.

I turned around. It was Tariq. What is he doing here? I thought. This wasn't his type of crowd. I smiled and walked over to him. Tina followed.

"What's up?" I greeted him with a hug.

"Long time no see," he responded playfully as he held me close.

He looked like a regular dude that day instead of a nerd like usual. He had on some baggy jeans that draped over a pair of fresh tan Tims, or butters as I called them. He had on an off-white long john shirt and a fitted cap that matched the Tims. My intentions were to flirt with him briefly and then go on about my business, but Tariq acted like he didn't want to let me go. "Where you been?" Tariq asked, still holding on to my waist.

"I been around," I responded as I gazed at the people passing by. I avoided eye contact with Tariq, as I was trying to see it all, not wanting to miss a beat.

"I haven't seen you in a while." He wanted to press the issue.

"You'll be seeing a lot more of me after tonight, babe," I said with a smile as I kissed him on his cheek. I was trying to keep the conversation short so Tina and I could continue to see and be seen.

"What are you doing after this?" he asked.

At the time I didn't have any definite plans for after the game, but I was sure I would make some and they wouldn't include being with Tariq. Not that there was anything wrong with him, I mean he was paying my mortgage. It was just that I was in the mood for something different, something new.

"I'm not sure just yet. Tina'll probably drag me to something," I told him.

"I want to see you this evening," Tariq said in a rather demanding tone. "So make sure you call me when you get done being dragged around by Tina."

"All right," I said. "I'll see you later."

I kissed Tariq on his cheek once more and slipped back into the crowd. I made it my business to go all the way to the other side of the building before I started hollerin' at dudes. I didn't want Tariq to see me in action. Shit, I didn't need to give him any excuses to stop paying my house off. Tina and I walked up on these fly dudes. It was three of them. One had on a throwback, some jeans, and some sneaks and a hat that matched the jersey. The second one had on a baby blue mink, a baby blue and white Sean John sweatshirt, some dark blue jeans, and some baby blue, dark blue, and white sneaks. The third one had on a tan long-sleeve T with a picture of Bob Marley on the front, some jeans, and some Tims. His accessories brought out his outfit—an iced-out Breitling, a platinum chain with an icy L, and a pair of studs that had to be at least two carats each. Throwback was light brown with big hazel eyes that locked on mine and followed my every move. Tina was on Baby Blue Mink, who was dark-skinned and stocky. Iceman was caramel-colored with dimples. I was on him too. I wouldn't have minded having him and Throwback.

Tina and me stopped in the flow of traffic and walked over to the side to introduce ourselves.

"You might as well put my number in there while you at it," Tina told the guy with the blue mink on as he was pressing buttons on his two-way sidekick.

"Oh, I'm two steps ahead of you, shawty. What it is?" Blue Mink asked with a heavy southern accent.

Tina recited her cell number. Meanwhile, I started talking to Throwback. We first exchanged names and numbers. Then we had a brief conversation about my outfit and how good I looked in it. After a couple laughs and flirtatious comments, we parted ways. We couldn't be standing around with niggas for too long because there were too many more ballers that we wanted to get acquainted with.

From what we saw when we weren't in the hall, the game was pretty good. We had court-side seats too, so that made it even better. We got to see all those fine- ass athletes up close and personal. Kobe Bryant did his thing, despite the crowd's boos. And A.I. put on a good show too. But I must say, I was more excited to see Michael Jordan play. In his whole career I had not seen him play. It took for him to come out of retirement and be in an All-Star game for me to see him live. But I'm glad I finally got the chance. After the game ended and the MVPs were announced, people flooded the halls once again. Tina and me took our time getting to the exit because we wanted as many people to see us as possible, especially outside when we stepped into the Hummer. Girls were dressed in tight miniskirts and see-through shirts, freezing their asses off for attention, and were pissed off when niggas looked past them to see who the two pretty bitches were gettin' into the Hummer. Tina and me were crackin' up. We had the driver turn the radio up real loud, and we had the windows down. We were sipping on Cristal, nasty and all just to see the look on bitches' faces. Niggas were walking up to the window tryin' to holla, some were just staring, and others would just shout compliments to us. Overall, we stole the let-out. As you know, the let-out is just as important if not more than the game. It is when you truly see how people are holdin'. Because they can have on all the jewelry in the world, but if their wheels ain't right, then they really ain't doin' it. While we were making our way out of the parking lot, my cell phone rang. It was a

Georgia number. It wasn't surprising that I got a call from Throw-back so quick, being as though him and his squad were from Atlanta and probably would be headed back home the next day. Like most out-of-towners, they were basically lookin' to get some before they left.

"What's crackin', sexy?" Throwback asked me with his heavy southern accent.

"Who is this?" I asked, already knowing the answer. "Damien."

"Oh, Throwback, Blue Mink, and Iceman from Atlanta. What's up?"

He chuckled. "Damn, you on ya job, ain't you?" "Basically," I replied.

"Well, don't worry, shawty, 'cause me and my boys ain't finnin' to rape nobody so you won't be needin' to give up no descriptions, ya heard."

"Oh, that's the least of my worries, trust me. Besides, those descriptions are for my records, not for no cops," I said.

He chuckled again and said, "You cute as you wanna be, you know that? I'm feelin' ya style, though." Then he popped the question. "What are yall gettin' into tonight?"

"That all depends on what yall are gettin' into." "Hopefully yall," he said, being honest.

I was horny just talking to Damien, and Atlanta was long ways from Philly, so a one-night stand wouldn't have hurt.

"If yall can find y'all way to my house, then it's a bet," I said flirtatiously.

"Give me the address," he replied.

The Three Moneyketeers, a nickname Tina came up with, found their way to my house. Tina and me had been waiting patiently. If we had pussies they would have been wet as shit when they pulled up in a platinum CLK 430 with twenty inches of chrome spinners. Got damn, I thought. Any plans of getting with Tariq that night just flew out the window.

Tina took Blue Mink and Iceman in one bedroom, and I had Throwback all to myself in my bedroom. Tina was great at what she did. She could easily handle two men without them getting the least bit suspicious about anything. She would say something like, "I like fucking with my skirt on" or "The only way in is through my ass." Guys would just take her for being kinky and go along with her, and it worked. Me, on the other hand, I had a hard enough time trying to do one dude without him seeing or touching something he would regret. Throwback was thrilled at my panties with the back cut out. He was even more thrilled that I had been willing to let him ass-fuck me the first time around. He was aggressive too. I had to make him stop a couple times. In bed he was opposite his subtle and sweet looks. He was like a raging bull. I guessed that was how he stayed so skinny. From that night on, the nickname Throwback stuck with Damien for more than one reason.

MARCH

March found me back in business. Tariq was still playing his part, even though our time together was more limited than ever before because I had been traveling a lot more pursuing my various long-distance relationships. O had been keeping tabs on me after he realized he wasn't the only cute motherfucker with cash. He had started spending more money on me, especially since he came up on a promotion. His opponent, the only other big-time dude in Delaware, had been killed, so O took over the whole state. Shawn was my getaway dude. Whenever I wanted to bounce, I called him and he would invite me on the road with him. He had been busy boxing, making money, and trying to be a champ. In the meantime, though, he sent me a credit card with a nice limit on it, and he made sure I never saw a bill. Throwback was my chat line buddy. We used up a hell of a lot of night and weekend minutes feeling each other out. We had become interested in each other on a different level than physical attraction. We liked each other's conversation.

Things were looking up for Tina and me. She had the boxer

Chris, the Puerto Rican hustler Jahuan, and she never did let go of white Derrek. They were all lacing her up.

I had just got back from New York from visiting Shawn. I hadn't seen O in a week, and he had been blowing up my phone. I decided to get with him to keep him from trippin' out on me. He had become so possessive.

He came to my house instead of me taking the trip to Delaware. That was a hell of a day. O looked good as usual. He had on an Enyce sweat suit and a fresh pair of Air Force Ones. I knew he wanted sex off the bat. I could see it in his eyes. Plus, lately that's all he had been coming around for.

We sat on the couch, and he put in a DVD that he brought from home. It was a porno. At first I wanted to tell him to take it out and go the hell home. I was really losing feelings for him. And even though I knew that getting used was part of the game for both him and me, I was beginning to hate it. I mean, all the other guys I dealt with treated me with a little respect. They didn't just want sex. Tariq and I actually had romance in our relationship. And O used to be like that, but he been on some other shit for a while then and I had been getting bored with it. The only reason I didn't cut him off right then and there was because he was still paying the note on that Range Rover I had sitting outside. Needless to say, I watched the porno with him and kept my mouth shut.

"Take off your clothes," O demanded. He was taking control again.

"Take off your clothes!"

I started unbuttoning my blouse slowly. O must have been impatient because he ripped my blouse off before I got to the third button. I didn't know whether to be scared or what, but I stayed cool. He started kissing on my breasts. I had my hands on his arms to keep him from touching the wrong places. He was kissing me so hard and I was trying to keep up. Then he managed to get one of his hands free and he quickly grabbed between my legs. I jumped up.

"What's wrong?" he asked.

"I can't," I said, holding my blouse together. "I have a yeast infection," I blurted out in embarrassment. I couldn't think of anything else.

He reached out and grabbed my arm, pulling me closer to him.

"Enough is enough," he began. "Look, Celess, you remember me telling you about that time I spent locked up?" he asked, trying to feel between my legs again.

"Yeah, you made your mistakes, so what?" I said, still trying to keep his hands from roaming, not catching his meaning.

"So, it's okay. I knew what you was about from the beginning. But I'm into that," he whispered.

I stood frozen, nervous, and scared for my life. O had my dick in his hand and started stroking.

I couldn't even get into it because of how shocked I was. O was fucking gay. That was some shit. All I could think about was wait till I tell Tina.

"AAARRRHHH!" Tina screamed in the phone. "Tina, I could not believe it. I couldn't even cum I was so appalled," I said.

"So all this time he was hip to it?" "That's what he said."

"That's a damn shame. Can you imagine how many girls he's fuckin' that don't have a clue that he likes dick?" Tina said.

"I know," I said.

I must admit finding out about O did take a load off of me. That meant I was able to be myself around him. We started taking showers together and having more sex than ever before. Our feelings for each other grew stronger. And the money he was giving me doubled. I think subconsciously he was paying me to keep my mouth shut. But that was just fine with me because I needed him to keep his mouth shut too. Our relationship changed dramatically, though. We had gotten to the point where we said "I love you" every time we spoke. I was even considering being exclusive with him, which meant I wouldn't have had to worry about a nigga finding out about me and killing me, because it was surely getting difficult to keep my secret.

I found myself going to extreme measures to keep Tariq, Shawn, and Throwback from finding out. I actually told Shawn that I thought I was pregnant. I faked him out for a month, telling him that my period was late and shit. Tina said I should have kept him going for a little while longer and got abortion money out of his ass.

Throwback was easy to string along because he was so far away. All of our time together was spent on the phone. But it was Tariq who had become a problem. He kept pressuring me to commit to him. He wanted a more serious relationship. I wasn't up for one of those with him, because that would have made my secret even more difficult to hide. So I brushed him off. We been on and off for some time because of that. I didn't mind, though, as long as my mortgage was still being paid.

"What? What do you mean, you haven't received payment for the month of March yet?"

"Ma'am, it shows here that you paid for the month of February but not yet for the month of March and the due date was March first. It is now March twenty-ninth, so you're going into the month of April delinquent, which means that you'll owe two months on April first," the woman on the other end of the phone explained.

"Well, have I ever been late before, I mean, what is the penalty? Is there a late fee?" I asked, totally confused.

"Ma'am, are you the person responsible for paying this mortgage?"

"No. That's why I'm confused.

"Well, maybe you should contact the person who is respon-

sible for making these payments and have them send March's
payment along with April's."

"Okay." I ended the conversation. I was pissed. I called
Tariq.

"What's up?" he asked nonchalantly.

"I just got a phone call from the mortgage company.
Apparently you didn't pay for March yet."

"The last time we talked, you told me that you weren't ready
for a commitment," he said.

"Yeah, and?" I asked, frustrated.

"Yeah, and neither am I," he responded. "What the hell is that
supposed to mean?"

"I'm not committing myself to nobody's mortgage who can't
commit herself to me," he said.

"You know what, Tariq, that's low. You could have called me
and let me know that you were going to stop paying my fuckin'
mortgage. I mean, you was paying it all this time and I wasn't
committed to you."

"Well, maybe I was trying to get you to commit," he said, still
sounding calm.

"Okay, but when we spoke a thousand times after I told you
that I was cool, why didn't you tell me that you weren't going to
pay my mortgage? If that lady wouldn't have called me I probably
would have wound up owing a chunk of change, and what if they
would have put my ass out or something! That was real corny of
you! Shit! I can pay my own fucking bills. Just like I had you
paying my shit, I'll have another one of my niggas picking up
where you left off! Faggot!" I shouted right before I hung up the
phone.

I knew I went too far, but I was upset. He could have had the
decency to call me and tell me to start paying my own shit. Now I
had to come up with $4,500 in three days.

"Tina, I need a favor," I said, still sounding pissed. "What's the matter?" Tina asked, concerned. "Fuckin' Tariq didn't pay my mortgage for March,"

I told her.

"Well, call his ass up and tell him about his self," she said.

"I did. He's not fuckin' with me no more, so..." "He still trippin' over that commitment bullshit?" "Basically, but I need forty-five hundred dollars by the first."

"Come get it tonight. I'll be back in Philly by like nine," she said.

"Thank you, girl," I said, relieved.

Tina was in New York with Chris the boxer. She had been spending more time with him lately. Jahuan had been put on the back burner. Tina hadn't even been going out with me much anymore. She was getting money, though. Chris was taking care of her and white Derrek was still sending her an allowance every week. Plus she still lived at home with her grandmom, so she didn't have any bills like that. Me, on the other hand, I had to spend a lot of the money I was getting from Shawn on my bills and the money from O on myself, so I really didn't have money to stash. But I knew Tina would have my back if I ever needed anything. I went to Tina's row house on Delancey Street that night. Tina had just got back from New York. She led me to her room in the basement of the house. She dug through her pile of pocketbooks and picked up a Dooney and Bourke duffel bag. She scrimmaged through the bag and pulled out a handful of balled-up money. I sat on the edge of her queen-sized bed and watched her unfold the money one bill at a time. She counted $4,000 in fifties and hundreds and then reached back into the duffel and counted out another $500.

"Why do you have your money balled up like that?" I asked.

Tina had a malicious smile on her face and said, "Girl, I stole this."

"From where?" I asked.

"Chris," she said, as if I should have known.

"You crazy! Why didn't you just ask him for it?" " 'Cause he's overdue already. I been accepting IOUs for the longest. He stingy as hell, always talking about he don't have no money."

"He gonna kick your ass when he find out." I joked. "Despite his career, Chris is a lover, not a fighter.

Plus, I'll put it back," she said with confidence.

I was with O when I got an emergency phone call from Tina. It was just two days after she lent me the $4,500.

She sounded breathless and it was hard to hear her, but I made out that she was at Methodist's emergency room.

"O, I gotta bounce," I said. "What's going on?" he asked.

"I don't know, my girl is at the hospital and I have to get there," I said frantically.

"The wrong nigga probably found out what was really under her skirt." O couldn't think of anything better to say.

I was heated. "O, you lucky you high 'cause I would fuck you up right now," I said to him.

"What?" he asked, as if he had no idea what I was pissed for.

"That was some fucked-up shit to say," I told him. O dropped me off at the hospital. They had just got Tina settled in a room. I was allowed to go back. When I walked in that room I didn't know what to do. Tina's face was three times the normal size. She was bruised badly. I threw my palms over my face and ran over to her.

"Oh, my God, Tina, who did this to you?"

Tina could hardly open her mouth to speak. Her top lip was so big it completely overlapped her bottom one. I held her head in my arms and tried to keep from crying.

"Over a couple dollars," she mumbled.

I know this may sound crazy, but I was relieved when Tina said that. It would have scared the shit out of me if this had been about one of her dudes finding out about her like O had suggested.

Tina stayed in the hospital for two days until the swelling went down. The police asked her if she wanted to press charges, but she said no. Her exact words were, "And get killed next time? Please." I took her to my house. She didn't want to go home. She was scared Chris would be there waiting for her. She stayed with me for about a week.

I finally got the whole story. Tina had been stealing money from Chris all along. She had been telling me that he been hookin' her up. But apparently he wasn't as loose with his money as most of the guys were that we dealt with. He was the stingy type, and Tina wasn't having that. I asked her why she didn't just cut him off and find a replacement, and she said that it was sweeter rippin' him off. That was Tina. She had the craziest logic.

APRIL

The alarm clock went off at exactly five-thirty. I was definitely not used to waking up that early. I had to force myself out of bed. Tina was already in the shower. I ate a bowl of cereal and got dressed. Tina was ready at six sharp, bags packed and everything. I found myself rushing, trying to be out of the house on time to get her to the airport by seven.

"Does he have all of your flight information?" I asked as we drove through the empty early morning streets.

"Yeah," Tina said.

"I'm gonna miss you!" I whined.

"I'm gonna miss you too, girl, but I gotta get out of here," she said.

"I know."

"That's all right, because I'm gonna be sending for you like every other weekend."

"Then I'm gonna be forced to deal with Terry," I said with a frown.

"I don't know why you don't like Terry, he's perfect for you," Tina said.

"He's OLD and BALD," I exclaimed.

"Yeah, but he's rich and he gets down the way you do."

"But that's the problem. I need a man, not a bitch. I'm the bitch."

"What do you mean?" Tina quizzed.

I looked at Tina with confusion in my eyes. "I didn't tell you?"

"Tell me what?"

"Terry likes it up the butt."

"Oh, my God! No, you didn't tell me!" "Girl, *I* was fuckin' *him*!" I explained. "Oh, my God!" Tina laughed.

"That's the only way he could cum. I begged him to put it in me, but he wasn't into that," I explained. "Um, um, um. Well, I'm glad Derrek ain't like that." Tina's face looked a lot better, but she still had bruises. She was wearing a pair of big Gucci glasses to cover her eyes and the tops of her cheeks. Her top lip was still swollen but a whole lot smaller than what it was in the hospital. She acted as if the incident with Chris didn't bother her, but I knew it did. I didn't try to beat anything out of her, though. I just decided to be there for her.

"Awww, take care of yourself," I moaned as I hugged Tina tight.

Tears were forming in my eyes. Even though Tina wasn't going to be gone forever, the thought of her leaving me here in Philly to fend for myself was scary, especially with all the drama that was going on.

"Don't you dare cry. We gonna be on the phone every day like normal," Tina said. "And we gonna see each other at least twice a month, I swear," she continued.

I gave Tina one last hug and watched her walk off into the airport. I got back into my car and drove off. I was on my own.

Tina called me as soon as she got to L.A. to let me know she was safe. Derrek was happier than a cat in a birdcage to have her there with him for such an extended period of time. He got on the phone and joked that I better get on the plane and come out there too because Tina was never coming back. I just giggled. With Tina gone, I had a lot of time to think. There were no parties, concerts, or bars to distract me. Tariq was out of my life, so I had no cuddle buddy, and O was busy getting high and sellin' dope. He was at a point where he was moving sixty thousand pounds a week. He had money in five states and twelve cities. He had houses in Delaware and one in Jersey, a town house in D.C., and a loft in New York. I was sure he had girls in all of those places too, or maybe boys, who knew? But I didn't care. He was paying all my bills and maintaining my wardrobe. I couldn't complain.

I spent one Sunday afternoon reminiscing and putting things into perspective. I got up out of my king-sized poster bed and dragged my feet across my mink rug. I went into my walk-in closet and retrieved some photo albums from an old suitcase I had hiding behind all my clothes. I pushed a pile of shoes to the other side of the closet and sat in the middle of the floor. The first album I opened had pictures of me when I was just a baby. Times my mom and dad took me to the zoo and the circus or just times we all spent at our house. There were pictures of me in the bathtub, taking my first steps, all the way up to me on my first bike. I just smiled at the sight of myself so young and innocent. Those were the days, I thought, when life was so simple, when my mom and dad were happily married, before I started messing shit up. It made me cry.

I wished I could go back to those days. Nobody even knew I was gay, except for my dad, according to my mom. She said my dad knew something was wrong when I started having more girl friends than guy friends and when I showed a strong interest for fashion. She claimed that was the reason he left us. I'll never forget the day she told me that.

The week after graduation I had made up my mind about

dressing up, which meant I had to come clean to my mom about being gay. I went downstairs to the kitchen where she was making dinner. I took a seat at the little round wooden table. My mom ignored my presence, as she did most of the time after my father left. I picked up an apple from the fruit bowl that sat in the center of the table and asked my mom to pass me a knife so that I could peel it. That was my way of getting her attention. She didn't pass me the knife. Instead she told me to get it myself because she had to turn the chicken that was frying. I got up and went over to the drawer. I took a knife out, rinsed it off, and returned to my seat at the table. All the while my mom was standing in front of the stove, not once looking at me. I told her that I had something important to talk to her about. She turned around with a disgusted look on her face and asked what was it.

"Mom, you know my friend Tina, right?" I began. "Yes, Charles, what about her?" my mom asked in a frustrated tone of voice.

"She's really a guy, Mom," I revealed.

My mom's face frowned up. She asked, "Charles, what are you talking about? I'm trying to cook dinner here. And Sister Anna is coming to pick me up at seven for Bible study, so I really don't have time for foolishness."

On that note I decided to get it over with.

"Mom, I'm gay and I want to start living my life as a girl like Tina does."

My mom had a look on her face that I will never forget. It was an expression of anger mixed with confusion. "Charles, do you know what you just said to me?" she asked.

I nodded my head yes.

"You sound crazy. Don't you know that God will punish you for this?" she asked.

"Mom, there is no proof of that," I said.

"No proof? Son, it is in the Bible. What more proof do you need? God intended for it to be man and woman. Not man and man! And the *fact that you want to change your sex? That's taking it overboard. You might as well slap God across the cheek with your bare hands!"*

"I'm telling you this because you're my mother and I need your support," I whined. "Not so you could judge me."

My mom turned back around to face the stove. "No son of mine will sleep with other men. And no son of mine will live his life as a woman," she mumbled.

"So what are you saying, Mom?"

"I'm saying that I won't approve! As long as you're under my roof, you will be Charles, the boy God made you, and you will not have dealings with other men!" she shouted.

"Well, Mom, I made up my mind, and if that means I have to go live with Dad, then that's what I'll do," I said. My mom turned to face me again. She looked into my eyes. "Do you think your father would have you in his house looking like a woman? If it was up to him, you would have been sent away a long time ago," she said.

"What do you mean, I would have been sent away?" I asked.

"Why do you think your father left? He knew you were gay all along. He wanted me to send you away to boarding school or somewhere. I'm the one who defended you. I swore to him that you were just going through a phase. We had many arguments over it, Charles. And eventually your father put his hands up. He walked out on us because of you, Charles. And now, ten years later, you come and tell me he was right! I lost my husband defending you, and you prove me wrong..."

When my mom told me that, I was so hurt and so ashamed. I felt unwanted and unloved. I remember being suicidal for a while after that day in the kitchen with my mom. It was then that I packed up my stuff and left my mother's house. Tina let me move in with her.

Transitioning was difficult for me at first. Not the dressing-up part, dressing like a girl was so comfortable for me it took no time to get used to. But all the miscellaneous stuff threw me for a loop. Tina taught me that living as a woman took more than fashion and attitude. It took discipline and a hell of a lot of money. We first had to get several surgeries, which we needed money to pay for. That's why Tina took me down Twelfth Street on a Friday night and introduced me to trickin'. I was in complete shock that night. There were all these gay guys posted up on various corners, some dressed like thugs, others dressed like girls. There was a heavy flow of traffic too. Cars were riding through continuously, stopping and picking up tricks. I was scared as hell the first night out there. I thought somebody was going to try to kill me, or an undercover was going to lock me up. Tina told me that I watched too much TV, and she assured me I would be fine. She said she had been working those corners since she was sixteen and nothing like that had happened to her or anybody she knew.

At that time it was obvious I was a guy and I was concerned that men wouldn't pick me up, but to my surprise more men wanted me than wanted Tina. And even more surprising, they were usually older, married men. In fact, my first, the man who broke me in, was married. I'll never forget him. His name was Ty. I offered to suck his dick like I did with every other guy that pulled up on me, but he insisted I let him fuck me. I explained to him that I was a virgin, but he was still with it. He said that turned him on even more. He was real gentle with me and despite the pain, I liked it—a lot. You can say I was turned out after that and not only by the sex, but by the money as well. He paid me three hundred, which was big change compared to the fifty to seventy-five I was used to getting off head. Ty was real cool, though. He showed me pictures of his kids and all. His oldest daughter was named Celess, which is how I got my name. I felt bad at first. But after six months of being out there I developed an I-don't-give-a-fuck attitude. Besides, Tina and me had no intentions on being out there forever like those other transvestites and cross-dressers. We had plans—big plans.

It took every bit of six months to make the money we needed

for our surgeries. By January 2000 we had silicone put in our chests, butts, and faces to get a womanly form. Tina had already been taking hormones, but I started on them after the surgeries. Ultimately, I had to change my diet, start exercising, and take all types of vitamins for my hair, nails, and skin.

After about a year, I was a totally different person. I had gone through a lot, but I was definitely happier as a woman. I didn't have to worry about being teased and looked at funny for being gay, like I had witnessed other gay men go through. I could walk around with a man and kiss him right in public without stares and hateful comments. That was probably the best advantage of dressing up.

I decided to call O after spending the whole day looking at old pictures, watching Lifetime movies, and crying. I finally got bored with myself. I wanted to get out of the house.

"Hey, O, it's me. Hit me back, I'm tryna see you," I said after the tone.

I waited for like an hour for O to call me back, and when he didn't I realized that I was due for a new dude. Anytime I didn't have a plan B, something was wrong. I got in the shower, threw on a royal blue and white J'adore sleeveless T, some Miss Sixty low riders, some royal blue stilettos, and a short royal blue leather jacket with cropped sleeves to my elbows. I grabbed my Dior clear-lens glasses and my blue Dior signature bag, and left.

It was a cool April night but nice. It was close to eleven o'clock. I went to Chrome nightclub on Delaware Avenue. It was somewhat packed. I peered through the crowd to see if I recognized anyone to socialize with. When I didn't, I walked over to the bar and sat down.

"What can I get you?" the bartender asked.

She was a tall white girl with long black hair that flowed straight down her back. She was very thin too. She looked like she could be a model.

"An electric lemonade."

Sitting there in Chrome alone made me miss Tina so much. I was used to her being right there by my side on nights like that.

"Damn, shorty, what's ya name?" a short, stocky guy asked.

"Naomi," I lied, which meant I wasn't interested. "You fine as shit, what you drinkin'?"

The bartender placed my drink in front of me. I paid her and picked it up.

"This," I told the guy as I extended the drink toward him.

"Well, I got ya next one, baby," he said. "That won't be necessary," another voice said.

"Oh, that's you, cousin?" the short, stocky guy asked. "My bad," he continued as he looked me over one last time and then walked away.

"Thank you," I said to the voice I had not matched with a face yet.

"No problem," the voice responded. "I knew he wasn't your type."

I finally turned around and asked, "What's my type?"

And damn it if my type wasn't staring me right in the face. He was light brown like honey with slanted light brown eyes and a head full of sandy brown curly hair. He looked good as shit. He had a gorgeous smile that revealed two tiny dimples and some beautiful teeth. I just wanted to jump on his lap and start tonguing him down. But I kept my cool, though.

"You look like you're into a good-looking guy who likes to have fun and spend money," he said, flashing that killer smile.

"Bingo," I said softly, unable to take my eyes off of him.

He smirked and introduced himself. "I'm Darrell." "Celess," I replied.

"Dance with me," he commanded.

And I did—all night, song after song. I thought I had fallen in love.

It had been three weeks since I'd been talking to my newfound friend Darrell and it had been at least that long since I'd heard from O. I called him almost every day and left messages on his phones. I wanted to make sure he was still paying my car note after the stunt Tariq pulled with my mortgage. He hadn't returned any of my calls. He hadn't even bothered to call me and check on me. I was heated.

"O, listen, if you got another girl or something just let me know. It's cool, you do your thing, I'll do mine. Just let me know what you're going to do about my car, that's all. You can fuck all the bitches you want. You can disappear for a month all you want. Just call me about my car, please!"

Ring! Ring!

Damn, I'm good, I thought, but it wasn't O. "Hello," I answered the phone quick.

"Hey, sexy," the voice greeted me.

I felt chills go up my spine. "What's up?" "I want to see you today," Darrell said. "Likewise," I said.

"Let's go down to the shore," he said. "The shore?"

"Yeah, we can chill at my beach house, maybe get something to eat, walk the boardwalk, see a movie..." "I'm sold," I said, smiling. I was into that romantic shit.

I hung up the phone with Darrell feeling giddier than a mothafucka. This dude is good, I remember thinking. Fuck O.

MAY

"TINA!" I said, crying.

"What the hell is wrong?"

"O!"

"Celess, calm the fuck down and tell me what is going on," Tina demanded.

I tried to stop crying and held back my tears. "They kidnapped O," I explained.

"Who? When? What happened?"

"I went to Delaware 'cause I ain't hear from him in a minute, and when I was ringing his bell the young bull that always used to be with him came up to me and told me he was missing," I quickly said in one breath.

"Well, when did this happen? I mean, do they know anything about who did it?" Tina sounded concerned. "Whoever did it was close to him and been planning it for a while, 'cause they snatched him up on 95.

He was making a major run to D.C." "How the hell they get 'im on 95?"

"He must have stopped at a rest stop, 'cause that's where they found his car," I explained. "All of the seats were cut open."

"Yeah, they knew 'im and they knew exactly what it was hittin' for. Anytime they know where his stash was," Tina concluded.

"I know," I said, sniffling. "And they got about forty thousand pounds and three hundred thou in cash."

"Them pussies made sure they wouldn't need ransom," Tina said, as if she was in thought.

I started crying again. "That's how I know they killed him."

I guess it wasn't "fuck O" after all, because I really got depressed after I found out about his kidnapping. It was weird that out of all the dudes I fucked with, I felt for O the most even though he was the one who brought me so much drama and treated me like shit sometimes. I didn't realize how much I felt for him until that shit happened.

Tina arrived at my house on a Friday afternoon. She had come to offer moral support. I was still in my pajamas in the bed. I hadn't been dressed since I last spoke to her on the phone five days before. I spent my days crying and thinking and crying some more. I couldn't help but think about all the brutal and crazy things they might have done to O or where he could be or if he was alive somewhere hanging on to his life. The thoughts I was getting were driving me crazy. I wished I could have done something. I just kept imagining him somewhere getting tortured or somewhere dead. I couldn't stop thinking or crying. "You have to snap out of this, Celess," Tina insisted. "Celess!" Tina sang as she waved her hand in front of my face. "You need to get in the shower, sweetie, and do something with yourself."

She sat down on the couch next to me.

"You need to find a way to get in his house," she continued. "He gotta have a stash at his crib. And find out where to send your car payments to before they come and repo that shit. You can get that new dude you got to pay the note. I don't know who gonna pay the insurance."

I just glanced up at her in disgust in between zoning out. Sometimes I wondered if she had a heart, or at least a conscience.

"Yup, I'm tellin' you, you should go back down to Delaware and see if somebody has a key. Oooh, no, call up a locksmith and tell them you locked yourself out. They'll make the key on the spot. You go in, find his stash, and roll out," she explained.

"Tina, please just be quiet," I finally said.

"Shit, it's just a matter of time before one of his fake-ass friends think to do it," she said, trying to justify herself.

"Maybe that's true, but O is out there somewhere probably getting fucked up or shot up or just lying somewhere dead, and you..." I burst into tears again. "Celess, I know you hurt and everything, but that's the game. Shit, I saw my whole family murdered behind that shit," Tina said with attitude. "After a while you just learn to suck shit up."

Tina could play tough all she wanted, but I knew walking in and seeing her mom, dad, and older brother dead in pools of blood cut her deep. She was only ten. Can you imagine seeing something like that at ten? She swears it had no lasting impact on her, but I'm not sure. The fact that she pretends like she doesn't care about anything or anybody is the result of seeing her murdered family's bodies at ten years old, among other things.

"Tina, it's easier said than done," I said, ignoring her façade.

"Well, be like Nike and just do it, hah!" she said, giggling, with a huge smile on her face. She slapped my leg in a joking, playful way.

"What DVDs you got?"

I just gave Tina a blank look and felt sorry for her. Tina's visit ended as awkward as it began. I was still depressed, and she gave up trying to make me feel better.

It was a rainy Monday. I had been sitting in the house all

morning contemplating what I was going to do about my car. I had the registration. It was in somebody named Carolyn Rodriguez's name. It had her address, so I decided to go to her house.

A short, chubby Puerto Rican girl came to the door. "Who you?

"I'm Celess, Omar's friend," I said, trying not to offend anybody.

"Mommy! *Una muchacha a la puerta. Una amiga de Omar,*" the girl yelled.

I waited at the door while a heavyset older-looking woman slowly walked down the stairs. She had long dark hair and a chubby face. She was wearing an oversized T-shirt that came past her knees and a pair of slippers.

"Come in, sit down," Carolyn said with a heavy Puerto Rican accent.

I walked into the small row house. "Hi, I'm Celess, a friend of Omar's," I introduced myself as I took a seat on the black leather couch beside Carolyn.

"Yeah, I know who you are," Carolyn said, looking me over. "Omar told me about ju. You one of the girls from Philly, right?"

"Yes," I replied.

"Which car you have?" she asked while motioning for her daughter to give her some papers from off the sixty-inch television in their tiny living room. "The Range Rover, the Escalade, or the Lexus?" she continued as she rummaged through the papers.

I was confused but I told her, "The Range Rover." "Right, right."

"Here is all the papers for the Range Rover, where you can make you payments to and everything, okay?" I took the pile of papers from Carolyn, but I stayed put on the sofa. I wanted to know more. It didn't make sense for me to take a half-hour trip in the rain and go back with no information.

"Did they ever find O?" I asked carefully. Carolyn looked at me, baffled. "Ju didn't hear?" "No, not really," I answered.

"Marisol, *espera en la cocina,*" Carolyn said to her daughter.

The girl left the room and headed for the kitchen. "The police came by here like a week ago because they found his car and it's registered to my address." Tears started to gather in Carolyn's eyes. She continued, "It was a robbery, they say, all of his seats was slashed and his trunk was open. They got his drugs and his money," she whispered. "But they couldn't find him.

"Then I got a call from a detective and he asked me all these questions about all the cars in my name. I told him Omar was my nephew. I raised him like my own, and when he asked me to put a car in my name as long as it's not illegal, I say yes," she spilled.

"Then like a day or two later the detective called back," Carolyn began, with tears forming again. "And they told me his body was found on the side of the highway. They say a wild dog brought it up from the woods. A highway patrolman saw his remains hanging from the dog's mouth."

Carolyn started to cry a little.

"They put the gun in his mouth and blew the back of his brains out, then they dumped his body in the woods off the highway. The police say if they would have found his body a minute later the animals probably would have eaten it."

"Did he have a funeral?" I asked.

Carolyn wiped her eyes and yelled, "Marisol! *Da me el papel de el frigorífico.*"

The girl brought her mother an obituary and returned to the kitchen.

"This is from the funeral. It was Saturday. They cremated him. His wife held a small memorial in Claymont," she informed me.

"Wife?" I blurted.

Carolyn schooled me. "Ju know what Omar was into, right? Ju

know how he lived. He had lots of girls. You think you were the only one, you crazy. That's why he bought so many cars and nice things, to keep all of you quiet, ju know that."

I just listened. She was right. I did know what O was into, just not as much as I thought I knew. I could have never guessed he was married.

"What about his house, can anyone get inside?" I asked, thinking about Tina's advice.

"Which one?"

"The one near here," I said.

"Oh, no, the police went there already and cleaned it out. It's boarded up now. He didn't have a stash there anyways," she said, hipped to my thoughts.

"No, he kept his stash in a safety box in one of them banks downtown. Only his wife has access to that. And he only stashed money here for me and my daughter, nothing for his girlfriends," she concluded. "I been getting calls from his udder girlfriends in Philly, but they not nice like you. They curse me out for telling them this stuff, for telling them the truth. But they need to hear it. They need to know that he's gone and he's not coming back and they need to find somebody else to take care of them."

I listened to everything Carolyn said. I took heed too. I had gotten closure, and now it was time for me to move on.

"Thank you so much," I said as I was walking out of the door.

"Ju welcome," Carolyn said. "Oh, here, ju can have this." She handed me Omar's obituary.

I took it and thanked her again. I got into my truck and drove off. I didn't cry. I actually felt better. At least I knew O had had a funeral and he was at peace.

JUNE

I was in desperate need of a vacation when Tina called to invite me to Cancún with her, Derrek, and Terry. I accepted without hesitating, and flew to Los Angeles on a Tuesday morning. That afternoon, Tina and I did some shopping on Rodeo for the trip. Derrek had given Tina a credit card with a $20,000 limit. We spent it in two hours. That's not surprising on Rodeo, where one item can cost as much as 20 Gs. We bought two pairs of sandals from Christian Louboutin and three from Louis Vuitton. We bought Versace and Dior bathing suits. We bought a pair of sunglasses for just about every outfit. Tina bought a $600 Anna Sui jacket just for the plane. It was refreshing shopping like that. It put me right where I needed to be emotionally.

Terry was already in Mexico on business, closing a deal on some investment properties in Puerto Vallarta. We were to meet him in Cancún on Wednesday. We expected it to be hot and steamy, but when we arrived we were surprised by how beautiful it was. We checked in at the Moon Palace, a gorgeous, prestigious resort. It was like a fairy tale driving through the big iron gates and having our names checked at the entrance. The marble floors and high ceilings were luxurious.

"*Hola,* welcome to the Moon Palace," a short, stocky Mexican man said as he gave us a cup half filled with red juice.

This was star treatment, I thought. We got our keys and caught a golf cart over to our suites. We had presidential suites. They were huge like houses. They had hammocks on the balconies that overlooked the pretty, tranquil ocean. It was like heaven. Terry wasn't scheduled to arrive from Puerto Vallarta until that evening, so I had my suite all to myself. Tina and Derrek said they were going to take a nap for a while and meet up with me when Terry arrived around seven. The first thing I did was get into the Jacuzzi. It was so relaxing, something I very much needed.

Knock, knock.

"Who is it?" I yelled, not feeling like getting out of the warm, bubbly water.

"Bags," the little Mexican voice yelled. "Come in, please," I yelled back.

Two short Mexican men entered my suite with a cart filled with my luggage. They unloaded the cart and placed my bags neatly along an empty wall in the foyer. I instructed them to take twenty dollars from my pants that I had lying on the floor and sent them on their way.

At a quarter to six, I heard the knob to my suite door turning. I sat up in the king-sized bed and looked toward the door. It was Terry.

"Heeey," he said with a huge happy-to-see-you smile on his face.

He was carrying a black briefcase, and a sports jacket was draped across his arm. I jumped up and ran over to him to greet him with a big hug.

"Long time no see," I whispered in his ear as we hugged each other tight.

I was not at all happy about seeing him, but it was the least I could do for his treating me to such a beautiful vacation.

Terry dropped his jacket to the floor and proceeded to put his briefcase in the safe.

"So how was the flight?" he asked, walking away from me.

"It was good, quiet," I replied.

"What do you think of this resort? Precious, huh?" he asked, looking at me with a grin.

"It's amazing. I can't thank you enough," I said, sounding like a little girl.

"Nothing but the best for you," he said.

I just smiled and returned to the bed. It had been a while since I'd last seen Terry—five months, to be exact—but nothing had changed. He was still old, still balding, still just plain unattractive.

"You know, I'm thinking about getting a house out here in Mexico. I've been down here for two weeks and I love it. And it's not far from my brother at all. L.A. is right across the border."

Terry had taken off his black loafers and walked over to the bed barefoot. He was wearing a white short-sleeved button-down-collar shirt, opened to reveal a white wife beater. He had on some black slacks, which he took off almost immediately.

"I missed you," he said as he slid onto the bed, positioning his back against the headboard.

"I told Tina to bring you to my brother's to stay for good," he said, still smiling.

I just blushed. "I have a lot going on in Philly, I can't just pack up and leave."

"Well, I'm glad you're here now. Who knows, you may change your mind about leaving Philly," he said with a grin.

Terry got comfortable and motioned for me to suck his dick. I started stroking his manhood and pumping myself up to get into it. I licked the tip a little to tease him. Then he pushed my head down, forcing his dick into my mouth. He began to really get aroused. He started taking my clothes off slowly. I felt the bulge in my panties growing. I had to think about my old fling James to make that happen. The best sex I ever had was with him. Terry started moaning and groaning. He was a girl trapped in a man's body, I swear.

"Come here, get on top," Terry said as he came out of his boxers.

I lifted my head up and sat on my knees. I took off my panties and started stroking my dick. Terry turned over on his stomach. I put some spit on my hand and rubbed it in on my dick to make the entrance easy. I slid in. Terry immediately started moaning. I started pumping up and down, in and out. Terry was excited. I had to rub on his dick to keep mine hard. Eventually he sat up on his knees, and we were going at it doggy style. I was beating his dick rapidly and pounding him from the back. I felt him getting ready to explode and I knew if I didn't get mine before he got his I would miss my chance of busting a nut, so I thought about James real hard and stroked Terry's dick uncontrollably.

"Oooh!" Terry blurted out as he came all over my hand.

I followed right behind him and it felt good.

Terry was a real freak. He started licking his cum off my hand. The next thing I knew, he was hard again and wanted more. This time he was satisfied with me sticking a dildo up his butt until he came. Lucky thing, because it was no way I would have been able to get up again so soon.

The next day came quick. Tina called me early in the morning to go to the spa with her.

"This hot-stone massage is the bomb." Tina squealed.

"I know, I needed this like crazy," I said. "I wish we could have gotten a full-body."

"Yeah, right. And take these towels from around our waists and let our dicks just hang out, huh?" Tina asked, not looking for an answer.

I frowned up my face at Tina and put my finger to my mouth, instructing her to shut up in front of the women who were massaging us. She laughed and reminded me that they didn't speak or understand English. "So, did Terry get plunged last night?" she asked with a devilish grin.

I rolled my eyes at her and ignored her sarcasm. "Well, all I know is Derrek tore my back out something nice in that suite," she bragged. "I'm surprised y'all didn't hear me."

"We were too busy making our own noise."

"Yeah, I heard you was packin'," Tina teased me. "Fuck you, Tina," I told her.

"Anytime," she said as she closed her eyes and smiled. She took a deep breath and said, "Isn't this a long way from home?"

I knew what Tina meant, and she was not talking about miles.

"Damn sure is," I agreed.

"I remember when I didn't have shit. Not a pot to piss in or a window to throw it out of," Tina recalled. "After those dealers killed my mom and them, and

I had to live with my grandmom, I didn't know what was going to happen with me. I just went buck-wild. "Started skipping school and smoking weed," she continued. "Then I got locked up for driving a stolen car. I was only thirteen. I was scared as shit. The judge told my grandmom it was up to her. She looked me in my face and said, 'The minute you start acting up again, I'm turning you in. The first day you skip school, I'm calling the judge.' I knew she wasn't going to turn me in for real, though, 'cause she wasn't tryna lose that check.

"I remember I left school early one day to go over this girl's house. I was walking under the bridge by myself and this old head pulled up to me and asked was I working. I didn't know what the hell he was talking about so I just kept walking. I went to cross the street and he pulled up in front of me, blocking my path. He jumped out of that little red car and grabbed me. I remember fighting him, but he was big."

I had heard this story a million times before, but it never stopped me from listening. Sometimes I thought Tina needed to tell her story in order to maintain her sanity. She'd been through a lot in her short life, which could be why she turned out like she did. Me, I had no excuses for being "confused," as my mom called it. I had both of my parents until they divorced when I was eight. I went to church every Sunday faithfully. I wasn't molested or raped. Growing up, I didn't even know anybody who was gay, male or female. I had what people would call a normal life.

Tina went on, "I was a little boy. He was a grown man." Then she began sniffling as if she was going to cry, but instead she wiped her eyes and smiled.

"But that's what got me where I am today, living the life. Just think, if I never got raped I would have never been gay. I would have been on the other end of the stick. Bitches would have been taking my money."

After our relaxing hours at the spa we had brunch on the beach. Afterward Tina and I did our daily exercise, and we all got dressed. Derrek and Terry rented motor scooters and took us into the city. We went to a theater and saw a play called *La Casa de Amor*. Ironically, it was about a Mexican madam who ran a popular and prosperous whorehouse. It was in Spanish, but the English translation was provided through a set of headphones given to audience members who requested them. We enjoyed it a lot. It reminded me of a soap opera.

Following the play, Derrek and Terry took us to a fine restaurant on the coast. It was a beautiful outdoor spot. The sun was setting on the horizon while we were being served our entrées, and suddenly but briefly Terry looked like a god. I felt so attracted to him. The setting was so romantic I couldn't help but feel the way I did. We ate grilled lobster tails and Spanish rice. Terry had Chardonnay, but the rest of us drank Zinfandel. Violins and flutes played while we ate. Some of the couples were dancing. It was just beautiful.

That night the four of us went to a private party in Guatemala. It was far from Cancún so we got rid of the scooters and took a helicopter over. A luxury sedan was waiting for us upon our landing. When we arrived at the party, I could not believe my eyes. Tina acted like she was used to the whole thing, but you would have thought I was seeing earth for the first time. I was in awe. We pulled up in front of a huge mansion with stone walls like a castle. There were valet parkers outside relieving men and women of their Bentleys, Rolls-Royces, and Aston Martins. Limos and Lincolns were pulling up and dropping people off. It looked like something from a movie. We walked up a lighted concrete path that led us to tall wooden double doors.

Tina and I were probably the only black people there, but it's what you wear that determines whether or not you fit in. And we definitely looked the part. Tina had on a black Donna Karan dress that was knee-length in the front but had a tail in the back that slightly brushed the floor. It had a slit down the front, exposing her cleavage, and her back was out. She was kind of chubby, but she wore the shit out of that dress. I wore a red Balenciaga silk-chiffon dress. It flared from my waist to my knees and was fitted at the top. It had rhinestone spaghetti straps. It was simple but very elegant. Both Tina and I were draped in diamonds, as were most of the women there.

"José!" Terry sang.

A thin, dark-complexioned Mexican man hugged Terry. They kissed each other on both cheeks.

"José, this is my beautiful date Celess, and my brother's beautiful date Tina," Terry introduced us.

We spoke and extended our hands. José kissed both our hands and then looked us over.

"Beautiful is an understatement, my friend. And to think I thought you guys were fags," José said with a laugh.

Tina and I kept our composures, as did Terry and Derrek. We all just chuckled.

Terry patted José on the shoulder and said, "This guy is a billionaire and still chooses to do stand-up." We chuckled again. José then excused himself and disappeared into the crowd. Terry and Derrek led Tina and me over to a sitting area toward the back of the house. We walked past four big rooms, which were set up like a restaurant. There were waiters and waitresses serving the guests.

"Nice, isn't it?" Terry asked.

"Oh, words cannot say," I said with a smile stretching across my face.

We all sat down to have drinks and talk. I couldn't lie: I was having the best time in my life. I actually felt like a million dollars. No Range Rovers, house payment, or shopping spree could compare to the treatment I was getting in Mexico.

"This house is huge, isn't it?" Derrek said as he lit a cigarette.

"Yeah, but where is the living room, dining room, and kitchen?" I asked.

"On the lower level, where the main entrance is," Terry jumped in.

"I thought those big wooden double doors were the main entrance," I carried on.

"No, sweetheart, that was the club entrance. You know that hill we rode up when we first got here? If you were to drive down it you'd see an off-road. That leads you to the main entrance," Terry explained.

"Damn," I said. "That's some hot shit."

"Ain't it, though. Long ways from Philly," Tina said, taking a puff from Derrek's cigarette.

"The man who owns this place, Cairo, his wife doesn't want for anything and she never lifts a finger. This is the kind of life I want to give to Tina," Derrek said.

Tina just smiled at Derrek's comment. I didn't think she knew how serious he was.

"You both deserve this kind of life, and you should let us give it to you," Terry said.

JULY

I got back from Mexico just in time for the Fourth of July. I checked my machine and there were no new messages. That was surprising. Things were a lot different without the three dudes I came into the game with. I didn't have anybody to chill with, and with Tina being gone I was bound to be miserable. I thought about calling Shawn, but since that incident with Tina and his bull Chris he hadn't called me, and I wasn't into chasing no nigga. The only other option was my new fling, Darrell. He was fine as hell and fun.

"Hello," a female voice answered.

"Hello, uh, can I speak to Darrell?" I asked hesitantly. "Darrell is out with the kids. Who's calling?" the woman asked, sounding just as confused as me. "It's Celess."

"Celess, I'm Rachel, Darrell's wife. What is this in reference to?"

"Nothing anymore," I said with an attitude.

I was so pissed that you would have thought Darrell been my man for years.

"Well, uh, what would it have been in reference to had I not been his wife?" she asked, returning the attitude.

I was in a shitty mood and this bitch wasn't helping any, so I decided to give her what she was asking for.

"This would have been in reference to us spending another beautiful day at his beach house, and another movie wouldn't hurt. Oh, yeah, and I would have definitely been in the mood for some of his homemade dumplings—"

She cut me off and blurted out, "Are you trying to say you fucked my husband?"

"No, your husband fucked me, even though I could have fucked him, seeing as how I have a dick," I shot at her.

"What? Wh-what are you talking about?" she stuttered.

I calmed myself and decided I was going too far. I was only with Darrell one time and it was no reason for me to put him out there like that to his wife. It wasn't her fault he was cheating on her, and he didn't know that I was a man, so I damn sure shouldn't have disclosed that information to her.

"Nothing! Never mind! I'm just pissed that he didn't tell me he was married," I said, trying to clean up my prior statement.

"I'm pissed too," she said. "How long have you two been seeing each other?"

"Since April, but we only had sex once," I admitted.

"That son of a bitch! He was with you while I was giving birth to his child," she mumbled.

I wasn't sure if I was doing the right thing by telling her so much, but it was fun airing his dirty laundry. I felt like it was what he deserved for being so stupid. "Listen, I'm sorry about all of this. I know you must be very hurt right now. But you don't have to worry about me calling Darrell anymore. I am through with him. Goodbye," I said.

"No, no, please, don't hang up." "Excuse me?"

"I want you to come over. Not today, because we're expecting guests. But one day next week. I'll call you. He's coming, I have to go, 'bye," she said in a rush.

I knew Darrell was too good to be true. That day at his beach house was probably something he did on the regular with a different girl every time. I didn't know why he would give me his house number if he was married, I thought. To be so cute, he was dumb as a damn doorknob.

I gave up on trying to hook up with somebody. I figured I'd lie around the house and watch movies to pass the time. But I just got bored with myself. I was lonely, and that was something I wasn't used to, especially on a holiday. I even thought about how nice it would have been to visit my mom. But I hadn't seen her since I left home almost four years ago, before I started dressing up. So I was not about to go around her like this, and she wouldn't have wanted me to either. Just when I thought I was hopeless, my cell phone rang.

"Yes," I answered. "What's up, sexy?" "Who is this?" I asked.

"Throwback," he answered, as smooth as can be. "Ohhh, hi," I said, remembering the night he got that name.

"You got plans for today?" "Hell, no," I said.

"Well, I'm in Philly, so let's hook up," he said. "Oh, sweetheart, you are a lifesaver."

Throwback came and picked me up, but this time instead of a platinum Benz, he was in a green Mercury Tracer.

"Tina, I can get past that the car didn't have leather seats or a sunroof. But the damn thing didn't even have AC! It was ninety-degree weather out there! I thought I was going to die! Talking about it's broke! I was heated! Literally! Then when I offered to drive my car, he said no!"

Laughing like she was watching an episode of *Martin*, Tina asked, "Why didn't he want to take the Range Rover?"

"This nigga talkin' about it's too flashy! He said if a girl was going to be with him she had to like him for him and ride with whatever! I told his ass that he might as well drop me back off because I wasn't the girl for him!"

"Girl, I'm about to cry, I'm laughing so hard," Tina said. "What did he say after you told him to drop you off?"

"Nothing. He dropped my ass back off."

"Well, what happened to the Benz?" Tina asked, still choking on her own laughter.

"It wasn't his from gate. It was his uncle's. The one that live up here."

Tina's laughing slowed up. "Well, what about the cute boy you just met, what's his name, David, Darnell?"

"Oh, my God, Darrell? Let me tell you about his married-with-kids-ass whose wife wants me to come over, for what, I don't know, but I'm guessing it's to see the look on his salty-ass face when he sees me and his wife chillin' together," I ran it down.

Tina just laughed some more. "Drama knows exactly where to find you."

"You ain't never lie," I agreed in a pitiful voice. "Aw, poor baby. What are you going to do?" "Be lonely like I was before all this shit," I said. "Aw, it'll be all right," Tina sighed.

"No, it won't. Come back," I sighed back. "If you was home, me and you would have tore the streets up today," I continued.

"I know, but..."

But what? When are you coming back? Chris is busy boxing, he ain't thinking about you no more," I pleaded.

"It ain't Chris I'm worried about. It's Derrek. He..." "He what?" I asked.

"He asked me to marry him," Tina said timidly. "What? Marry him? Whatever!"

"I'm serious, Celess."

"And did he give you a one-way ticket back home when you said no?"

"I didn't say no."

"What? So you are going to marry him?" "Yes."

I was surprised and mad at the same time. I think deep down inside I knew if Tina married Derrek she would definitely not come back to Philly, and that would hurt my heart. I mean, Tina was all I really had. She was my friend and my family.

"So when is this supposed to happen?" "We didn't set a date yet, but soon." "Um, um, um..."

"You mad?" Tina asked. She must have sensed it. "No," I lied. "If you're happy, I'm happy."

Tina knew I was bullshittin'. She started explaining herself.

"I'm just tired of playing the game, you know?" she said. "Derrek is perfect for me. He knows everything about me already and he's cool with it. Plus he got plenty dough and I know I'm safe with him. I can just chill. My worries are over with him—all of them, you know?"

As much as I hated to admit it, Tina was right. Derrek was her best bet. I was just jealous and lonely at that time. I was feeling left out. I mean, Tina introduced to me this game of dressing up and having dudes thinking I'm a chick, taking care of me. And now it would be like I was out here alone playing by myself.

"Well?" Tina asked, interrupting my thoughts. "Well, what?" "Are you still mad?"

I thought about her question and I realized that if the shoe was on the other foot, if somebody who knew all about me, who could take care of me, and who I was attracted to offered to take me away from all the stress and bullshit of going from man to man, I would take him up on it.

"No, girl, I'm not still mad," I said sincerely. "I just can't believe it. Tina getting married?" I pondered aloud.

"I know, right. It sounds crazy, but it's the best thing to do. I would be a damn fool to say no."

"You're right and I'm happy for you, for real," I said with tears in my eyes.

The clock said eight twenty-five. I turned over in my bed and reached for my ringing phone, wondering who could be calling me this early on a Monday.

"Hello," I said, sounding like I had swallowed a mouthful of sand.

"Hello, may I speak with Celess?"

I sat up, trying to figure out who the voice on the other end of the phone belonged to.

"Who's calling?" I asked, praying it wasn't any bill collectors.

"This is Rachel Greene, Darrell's wife," she answered. I took a breath. "What can I do for you?"

"I am so sorry to wake you. Darrell just left for work. Listen, I want you to come over to the house this evening so when he comes in from work, you'll be here and we can get to the bottom of this," she began.

"Rachel, listen, my part is done. I don't think I want to get any more involved in you and your husband's personal problems than I already have."

Rachel cut in quick. "I understand that completely, but when I confront him about you, he'll just deny it, and if I don't have solid proof, he'll just wind up getting away with cheating on me like he always does. You know how men are."

"I don't know..." I said.

"I need your help. I mean, us women have to stick together. You didn't know he was married. It's not your fault."

"I know, but..."

"He was obviously going to try to play you too," Rachel said.

She sold me with that one. "What's your address?"

I promised to be at Rachel's house by four-thirty. I figured, fuck it, I didn't have anything to lose. Plus, I couldn't wait to see what Darrell was going to do when he walked in from work and saw me in his house with his wife.

I made sure I looked sexy. I put on some Dolce & Gabbana

jean booty shorts, a white wife beater, and a pair of gold BCBG stilettos. I wore my gold Chanel jewelry and my white and gold Chanel bag. I pulled my hair back in a slick ponytail held together with a gold Chanel clip. I threw on my gold Chanel belt, put on my gold Chanel glasses, and left. I was fly.

It was four-thirty when I arrived at Rachel's. I parked the Range Rover on the corner of the block as planned, then walked down the street, passing three single homes to reach Rachel's. It was a brick single two-story home with vinyl sides. The grass was freshly cut and a small garden was maintained along the walkway. I rang the doorbell.

"Hiii," Rachel sang as she let me in her house. I gave a slight smile and said hello.

"Celess, it is nice to meet you," she said, looking me over. "Have a seat."

I sat down on a red fabric sofa neatly decorated with multicolored pillows. In front of me was a wooden coffee table with a glass top. There were issues of *Essence* and *Sports Illustrated* spread across it.

"Can I get you anything to drink—a glass of water, perhaps?"

"Yes, thank you."

I looked around the house. The walls were covered with family photos. From the looks of it, Darrell and his wife had three kids, two boys and an infant girl. I was disgusted that he never mentioned any of them. One thing I couldn't stand was a man who denied his kids. Did he think I wouldn't have dealt with him if he told me he had children? And if so, it's not that much good pussy in the world (even if I did have one).

"Here you are," Rachel said as she set the tall glass of ice water down on the table.

She sat down in a reclining chair to my right and crossed her legs. Rachel seemed very sophisticated and somewhat posh. She had pale light skin with big brown eyes and a big smile. She wore her hair down on her shoulders. It was bouncy and curled. She had on a dark blue jean skirt that came to her ankles with a slit up the side to her knee. Her yellow short-sleeve cotton shirt was tucked in neatly, revealing a brown leather belt. She had on some brown flip-flops to match her belt. A pretty face, but she was so simple. She was a plain Jane. She had nothing on me.

"You have a beautiful home," I said, trying to break the awkward silence.

"Thank you," she said, smiling, staring at me strangely. "We just did some remodeling right before the baby was born," she explained.

"How old is she?" I asked, referring to the baby girl in the pictures.

"She's going on three months. I had her on April twenty-first, the day Darrell had to close an urgent business deal, or so he said. But I'm sure he was at the beach house with you," she said, still smiling.

I almost spit out my water.

"We've been married for eight years, since we were twenty-four. We have two boys, Darrell, Jr., or D.J., he's seven, and Andrew, he's four, and now a girl, Danielle," Rachel volunteered.

"I always suspected that he was cheating on me, even before you, but I just couldn't prove it," she continued. "But he never slipped up like this before, giving out our home number. He must have felt comfortable with you calling here while I was in the hospital with Danielle. But that was still stupid of him," she said, thinking aloud.

I just sat there and listened, occasionally getting lost in my own thoughts, trying to figure out why the hell I was there in the first place.

We heard a car pull up in the driveway. Rachel stood up and walked toward the door. I sat up straight and became alert.

"It's him," she said.

"Hey, honey," Darrell said as he entered the opened door. Darrell kissed his wife on the cheek and gave her his laptop bag. She placed the bag in the closet by the front door as Darrell walked toward the living room.

"Who—who is this young lady, sweetheart?" Darrell stuttered, with a puzzled look on his face.

Rachel entered the living room behind him. "Don't you recognize your friend Celess? She phoned the house on Friday and we got to talking and I invited her here today so that we can get to the bottom of your infidelity issues," Rachel told her husband.

Darrell looked pissed off. "What did I tell you about snooping around in my business?"

"Honey, you're the one who gave her this number.

It's not like I went looking for her."

"Where are the kids?" Darrell asked, as if they'd just popped in his head.

"They're over my mom's."

"Oh, so you actually planned this confrontation?" Darrell yelled.

"Yes, I did. I'm getting sick and tired of you cheating on me!" Rachel began to get emotional. "And you had the nerve to do it while I was in the hospital giving birth to your daughter! You're sick!" Rachel said, as she hit Darrell in his chest with her balled fist.

Darrell gripped her by her arms and forced her into the kitchen. I just sat there and watched the whole thing like it was a movie. They were still arguing in the kitchen, but it was harder to hear them. I got up and walked over to a wall. I put my ear to it, hoping to hear better.

"Listen, you have to stop spying on me! That's why I cheat! If I didn't do anything, you would still accuse me, so I might as well do what I'm getting charged with!"

"What kind of logic is that, Darrell? You've been cheating

since forever! If I've ever accused you it's because you've given me reason to!"

It sounded like Rachel was crying.

"Oh, that's bullshit, Rachel, and you know it! When I *was* faithful you didn't trust me. You gave me hell about everything! And you wonder why I cheat on you. Look at the stunts you pull! Getting rid of the kids so you can invite a woman over to throw it in my face that you caught me!"

There was a brief pause.

"And you went all the way too! You went all the way this time!" Rachel yelled.

"What are you talking about?"

"A man, Darrell? What, did you think she had me fooled with those high heels?"

"What the hell are you talking about?"

I pressed my ear even harder against the wall. I wasn't sure I heard her correctly.

"I know your little girlfriend is a man! She told me on the phone. Plus it ain't that hard to tell. How could you not tell me you were gay?" Rachel screamed.

I didn't wait around for Darrell's response. I grabbed my bag off the couch and sped out of that house. I could not believe it. How could she tell? I wondered. I was insulted. I mean, I was not some typical transvestite or drag queen who wore women's clothes and makeup for entertaining purposes. This was my life, and I worked damn hard to achieve this look. What the hell did she mean, it's not hard to tell? I kept looking at myself in my rearview mirror to make sure my makeup was still intact. I didn't notice any flaws. I drove to a McDonald's on City Avenue.

"Excuse me, where's your restroom?" I asked, sounding pressed.

I walked into an empty stall. I looked down at my private area. Shit! I thought. There was a huge bulge in my shorts. How could I have overlooked that? I hurriedly unbuckled my belt and unbuttoned my shorts. I put my hands in my panties. My penis was no longer tucked in between my butt cheeks. The tape had come off.

"Shit!" I whispered.

I dug into my bag. No tape. I tried squeezing my cheeks together tight, but it wasn't working, either. I was so frustrated. I just had to hurry home and hope no one would notice from here to there.

I held my bag in front of me, trying to hide my secret, and slipped out of the restroom. Now I knew what a girl felt like when her period came on unexpectedly.

AUGUST

I t was a misty Wednesday afternoon. I was sitting on the
couch watching talk show after talk show, eating grilled hot
dogs, and drinking iced tea. I hadn't spoken to anyone all day and
wanted it to stay that way. I was spending nothing time with
myself and I actually enjoyed it, lounging around the house in
nothing but a T-shirt and a terry-cloth robe. I was comfortable.

From my window I saw the mailman leave mail in my box. I
got up from my warm and cozy spot on my couch and went
outside to see what bills I had. Lately, I'd been seeing more and
more bills, something I wasn't used to. To pay my mortgage and
utilities, I had been digging into the stash that I had been able to
accumulate when O started doubling the money he gave me. For
groceries and personal items like hormones, I depended on the
rent money I collected from the tenants who lived in the duplex
that Tariq bought me for my birthday. Tina helped out too,
sending me money every two weeks. At times she even sent me
new clothes and shoes, but that was because L.A. got styles before
Philly did, so she said she was just keeping me ahead of the girls
out here.

I skimmed past the junk mail and circulars and came across a cute decorative envelope with no return address. I went back inside, found my place on the couch, and opened the envelope.

Dear Friend,

You are a blessing from the Man up above. I remember when we first met. I was sitting in a classroom in Franklin waiting for the teacher to start the class and you came in and sat next to me. You smiled at me like you was going to holla at me. And I thought to myself, either he sees through me and knows I'm a guy or he thinks I'm really a girl and is trying to play the straight role. Either way, I knew you were gay. From that day on I took you under my wing and I taught you so well that later down the road you were better at the game than me.

Now, after seven years, you are all I have. You have been the only one by my side since. You have kept me level-headed and out of trouble and I appreciate you for that. I don't remember what it was like to have a family because it's been so long since I've had one, and when I did have one it was dysfunctional. It was hard finding unconditional love from a father who spent most of his life in prison, a mother who put crack before her own children, and an older brother who was too busy trying to follow in my father's footsteps, trying to be a drug dealer.

Anyway, it wasn't until I met you that I found that love—that kind of love you get from a family. I probably would have been lost without it.

I have changed a lot since I've been in L.A. with Derrek. I am a different person. I forgive my family and I forgive the pervert rapist who introduced me to homosexuality. I forgive my grandmother who let me live in her house but who didn't give a shit about me. And most importantly, I forgive myself for hurting so many people and playing with people's sexuality. And that's why I'm writing you. I want you as my friend to get out of the game. I want you to stop faking dudes out for your own sake and theirs. You know like I know that it is not fun being gay. Nobody wants to be gay. And to force that lifestyle on a straight man is wrong. I finally see that. There is a man out there who

*is gay by choice and would love to give you the world, so please wait for
him to come along.*

*Plus, I wouldn't want to see anything happen to you. You mean a
lot to me. Also, Celess, please contact your mom. Be in touch with her,
because you only get one. I know she couldn't handle your being gay
and cross-dressing, but at least do your part and keep in touch with her.
You are her only child and you two only have each other. With all that
said, I love you dearly.*

Love ya, girl,

Tina

*P.S. I know you are wondering what the hell Derrek did to me. The
answer—he showed me what love really was.*

Tina was right, I *was* wondering what the hell Derrek did to
her. I closed up the letter and then read the invitation that was
placed inside it. Tina and Derrek were getting married at the end
of the month in Albany, New York. There were two round-trip
train tickets stapled to the invitation. I sat back and reread the
letter. I was trying to imagine Tina writing it. I couldn't see her
sitting down and writing a letter, period, much less those words.
I took it all in, though, and started to feel mushy. I mean, I was
happy that she was truly my friend and that she felt the way she
did about me. Just like she didn't have anybody else, I didn't
either, even though my family was alive. But on the flip side I
was upset that she would come out of the blue and ask me to
stop doing what I was doing. I mean, back when I was feeling
bad about it she was the one telling me to get over it. Now that
she found somebody and she was out the game, suddenly she
cared about people's feelings. So what did she expect me to do,
get a job and start paying my own bills? Start frequenting gay
bars looking for Mr. Right? Please. She had some nerve, I
thought.

I put the mail to the side and finished watching my shows. I
laughed at parts that weren't even funny, trying to keep my mind

off of Tina's letter. I tried pushing it to the back of my mind. But it was impossible.

Who was she to tell me to reconcile with my mom when she lived with her grandmom for I don't know how many years without even saying hi and goodbye? She was the one who told me to hell with my mom when I cried for three days straight after she told me she didn't have a son anymore. And she said she forgave her grandmom. For what? Her grandmom didn't do anything except let her do anything she wanted to. No matter how hard I tried, I couldn't get Tina's letter off my mind. It was tripping me out and I wanted bad to call her, but I knew I wouldn't have had the heart to say to her any of what I was thinking. So fuck it, I thought. Fuck the letter and fuck how she felt. Fuck her being a new person. I wasn't about to have food taken out of my mouth because she found her conscience. And when did the wizard start giving out consciences, anyway? Shit, she should have gotten a brain, because she must be real stupid if she thought I was getting out the game.

It took about a week for me to completely get over the message I got from Tina, and I had to take yoga classes to do it. I just took the letter for what it was worth. In the meantime, I developed a love for yoga. It not only took my mind off of things, but it also occupied my time, which I had a lot of since I was without a man. "Now breathe," Debbie, the yoga instructor, said softly.

I was stretched across the floor surrounded by about seven women and two men. We were all in tights and T-shirts. I wore my T-shirt to the middle of my thighs, unlike the other women, who wore baby Ts or sports bras.

"Now pull...Now release."

The room was completely silent except for the deep breaths. Everyone was concentrating and in their own worlds. It was calming.

"Okay, class, that's our time," Debbie said as she slid from her lying position to her knees.

"I'll see some of you Friday and the rest of you next week."

After class we all gathered our belongings and scattered. As I left, one of the women, someone new to the class, approached me.

"Great class, I can always go for yoga."

"Yeah, it definitely does your body good," I said, not knowing what else to say.

"Yeah, forget about milk, right?" the pale-skinned lady said, winking a big green eye. "I'm Sue Ellen." She freed her hand from her gym bag to give me a shake.

"Celess," I said. "Nice to meet you."

"So how long have you been taking this class? Is the instructor any good?" Sue Ellen asked with a smile. She seemed happier than any average person on any average day.

"For about two weeks now, and yeah, she's pretty good."

"Well, uh, listen, I'm headed to Reading Terminal for lunch, you wanna join me?"

I was hungry, so even though Sue Ellen struck me as one of those types who could get on your nerves with all of her talking, I accepted the invitation. I figured a little lunch couldn't hurt.

Sue Ellen and I walked a few short blocks to Reading Terminal. Center City's streets were crowded and busy, since it was lunch hour. Inside Reading Terminal, which looked like a mall food court, we got our orders, then grabbed seats at one of the few tables available.

I was happily putting a dent into my cheeseburger and paused when I realized Sue Ellen was looking at me the entire time.

"Here I am eating a cucumber salad and looking like a house and you're chomping down on a cheeseburger with the works looking like a model. How is that?"

I smiled and said, "Genetics," and continued chewing.

Sue Ellen kept her eye on me throughout lunch. I thought maybe that's what white people do and over-looked it. Occasionally I would look up at her and smile. Then I decided to stir up a conversation about class.

"So what gave you the urge to try yoga?" I asked, sipping my root beer.

"I was in a bad car accident a little while back and my doctor recommended it, you know, for therapeutic reasons," Sue Ellen explained between chewing a fork-full of cucumbers.

"Oh, well, I hope it helps," I said.

"Yeah, me too. God knows I need to get rid of my back spasms. What about you? Why did you decide to take the class?"

"Honestly, it was a mix of being bored and needing to get my mind off of things," I responded.

I kept the conversation going to avoid the awkward silences and stares by Sue Ellen. Then, as we were parting ways that afternoon, I found out what her stares were all about.

"It was a pleasure, Sue Ellen," I said, ending our lunch.

"Oh, believe me, the pleasure was all mine," she said. I was taken aback by her enthusiasm.

"Well, I guess I'll see you again in class," I said as I stood up from the table.

"Or maybe we can see each other tonight for dinner. I'm great in the kitchen and"—Sue Ellen giggled— "in bed."

First I was speechless. Then I was motionless. "Excuse me?" I asked as if I hadn't heard her.

She wiped her mouth with her napkin and stood up. "You know," she said as she licked her tongue out at me in a seductive manner.

"Oh, my, um, Sue Ellen, I'm sorry, but you have me mistaken. I don't date women at all," I said firmly.

"No kidding? Well, I am sorry. It's just that you're so masculine, I thought..."

I'd like to have slapped the hell out of Sue Ellen, but I just laughed it off. It must have been the over-grown T-shirt and the clunky track sneakers I was wearing. Whatever, the incident with Sue Ellen reminded me that I needed a man.

"Hi, I'm responding to an ad in the paper, SBM looking for SBF—" I said reluctantly.

"Yeah, it's me," the deep voice cut me off.

"Hi, how are you? My name is Celess," I said, trying not to laugh.

I was all giggly inside, like a girl being introduced to her first crush.

"Hey, Celess, I'm Michael. I'm surprised someone responded," he said.

"Yeah, I'm surprised I was that someone." There was a pause.

"So, Michael...what do you do for a living?" I asked. Apparently I was going to have to initiate the conversation.

"I'm an architect. I get contracts for universities, hospitals, and things like that. What about yourself?" he asked, sounding professional.

"I'm a...yoga instructor," came sliding off my tongue.

He caught me off guard. No man had ever asked me that who I was interested in enough to lie to.

"Um, that sounds interesting," Michael said.

"But my ultimate goal is to open my own hair salon," I quickly added to throw him off.

"Hmm, a yoga instructor and a hairstylist? Sounds like you're pretty well rounded," Michael said.

"I guess you can say that," I said before changing the subject. "What part of the city are you from?" I asked. I was trying to gather some background information on Michael. It was easy and probably very likely to be deceived when hooking up with people who placed ads in search of companionship.

"Well, actually I'm from Boston. But I live in South Philly on Columbus Boulevard. I've been here for two years now," he answered.

"How is it living on that strip? It must get loud on the weekends with all those nightclubs."

"Actually, it doesn't. For starters, I'm on the twenty-fourth floor, so—"

I cut him off and said, "Oh, you're in those lofts down there on the water. You must have an amazing view."

"I do, yes. I see the Delaware River from my living room and the skyline from my bedroom. It's something to see at night.

"What about you? Where do you stay?" Michael turned the interrogation on me.

"I live in a town house myself, right off of the main line," I told him proudly.

"Do you have any children?" he asked.

It was funny how men first wanted to know if a woman had children and women first wanted to know what a man did for a living.

"No. Do you?"

"I have a seven-year-old son," Michael said.

Although I was disappointed, I said, "Well, I can't wait to meet him."

"Well, he lives in Boston with his mother. My job requires me to do a lot of traveling, so we agreed it was better and more stable for him to stay with her," Michael told me.

I was relieved. I mean, it wasn't that I had a problem with children. It was just that I wanted no parts of a man's baby's momma drama.

"So, I'm curious...Celess, right?" "Right," I answered.

"What made you respond to my ad? I mean, I'm pleased that

you did, don't get me wrong. But it sounds like you have things in order. You shouldn't have a problem getting a man."

"If that is your way of asking if I'm ugly, then no, I am not. In fact, I'm very attractive. I would even bet that I look better than any woman you've ever dated, including your son's mother," I said with sass.

"Ohhh," Michael said. "We'll just have to see." "What about you, mister?" I teased. "Why did you even place the ad? I think that's a more desperate move than me responding to it."

"To be quite honest, I've been in Philadelphia for every bit of two years and I have not found one woman that I could see myself in a relationship with. I guess I do sound kind of desperate, then, huh?" Michael chuckled. "No, but really, I've been on a few dates, and the women either didn't click with me or weren't my type, or one time it turned out that a woman was with me for my money," he continued. "So I placed the ad. Now tell me, why did you respond?"

"I responded to your ad because I'm tired of picking up men at clubs. Well, that and because another woman offered me sex today as if I had the words *lonely* and *horny* tattooed on my forehead," I answered honestly. Michael and I shared a laugh at our seemingly desperate selves. We ended up talking for about two hours, getting to know each other better. We ultimately made plans to have dinner the following day. I was anxious to see what he looked like and prayed it was every bit of the six-foot, brown, muscular description he placed in the ad. It was a beautiful evening. The air was thin. It wasn't as humid as it had been for the past couple days. Delaware Avenue was lit up and busy. I was dressed in a chic black BCBG shirt and skirt, with black leather BCBG open-toe stilettos and a black Gucci clutch. My hair was pulled back in a bun, and I went modest on the jewelry: some platinum and diamond studs in my ears and a platinum and diamond bangle. I wore a black flower on my neck, so a necklace was unnecessary. I was going for the sophisticated, sexy look. From the parking garage I took the elevator up to Hibachi. "Hello, reservations for Michael LaBlanc," I said to the hostess with a polite smile.

The short Asian girl scanned the reservation list. "Yes, right this way," she said as she led me to a two-person booth in a secluded spot in the restaurant.

Hibachi was casual but classy. It had nice Asian- influenced decor. That night all of the attendees were dressed up and looked wealthy.

"You must be Celess," Michael said as he stood up to greet me. He kissed me on the hand gently. "Pleased to meet you."

"Likewise," I said, smiling.

"I have to say, when you described yourself over the phone, I thought to myself there's no way she can be this beautiful, but wow, you're even more beautiful than you described," Michael commented.

I blushed something terrible. "Thank you," I said. Michael was good-looking too, but in a different way than what I was used to. He didn't have the cute-as-a-motherfucker sexy-ass thug look like O, James, and Darrell, and he didn't have the mature, handsome look like Tariq. He had an actor's look. His body was very well maintained and athletic. He had a perfectly shaved head and face. He was just all right in the face, even a little on the unattractive side, but there was something about him, his demeanor, his poise, that captivated me. "Hello, can I start you two with something to drink?" the waitress asked.

Michael motioned for me to order first. He was a perfect gentleman.

"I'll have a water for now," I said, skimming through the menu.

"And you can bring me a flaming volcano," Michael said.

The waitress punched our requests into a handheld compu and took off.

"You look very nice," Michael said, looking me in the eye.

"Thank you," I said redundantly. "You look nice yourself."

"Thanks. Are you hungry? Because I'm starved," he s opening his menu.

We ordered our appetizers and entrées, and before we kne we were ordering dessert.

"This has been a wonderful evening," Michael said as walked hand in hand out of the restaurant.

At that point I was a little tipsy off of the volcano Mich convinced me to order. I was full of laughter and corny jokes.

"An evening full of wonder, yes," I agreed.

Michael laughed. "I haven't had a date like this in a lo while."

"You and me both," I said, stumbling out of the door.

"Where did you park?" Michael asked, holding me up by waist.

"Valet, the only way," I said. "Ooh, that rhymed. I should b rapper," I added.

I started searching through my purse for my ticket. "I th you had too much of my volcano," Michael finally realized.

"No, that volcano had too much of me," I said with sass.

I pulled my ticket from my purse and gave it to the parking va

"Are you going to be able to drive home?" "Better than I' able to walk," I said.

"I think you should let me drive you to my house until morning. You're pretty messed up," Michael suggested.

"Are you planning on taking advantage of me?" I sang fl tiously as I played with the button on his Polo shirt.

"Not at all. I mean, I'll drive you home and take a cab b you want," Michael said.

"You don't drive?" I asked, confused.

"Well, I do own a car, but I drive very little. Only when I'm going to Boston or somewhere far from my house," he answered.

"Oh, 'cause I was about to say, you have to have a C-A-R if you want to be with me."

"Isn't it J-O-B?" Michael asked, referring to the song. "Isn't what J-O-B?" I asked.

"Yeah, I think I will drive," Michael said.

I woke up with a pounding headache. I looked around the room and thought I was lost. I looked down at the bed I was lying in and panicked. There was no one beside me, but I wasn't in my bed. Then it hit me. I was in Michael's house and oh, my God, I was not wearing my clothes. I started touching my private parts to make sure they were still intact. I was in a pair of oversized shorts and a T-shirt. Who put these clothes on me? I wondered. I jumped up, still scared. Michael couldn't have helped but discover my secret if he had undressed me. I tried hard to remember what went on, but the last recollection I had was in the restaurant. I decided to hurry up and get out of there, but just as I attempted to get out the bed, Michael came into the bedroom. He was carrying a tray with a large knife sitting on the edge of it. I didn't look at his face to catch his expression because I was too busy keeping my eyes on the knife. I was nervous as all hell. And all I could think about was him chopping my penis off with that knife. I had to get out of there.

"Michael, please don't, I'm sorry, but..." I pleaded as I eased out of the bed.

Michael looked at me, baffled.

"Celess, what's wrong with you? I'm not going to hurt you. I made you some breakfast," he said as he sat the tray of food down on the nightstand. "Here, let me take that. I was chopping onions," he said as he removed the knife from the tray.

I paused. I was really trippin'.

"Promise me you will not drink another flaming volcano ever in your life. You're bugged out," Michael said with a smile. "Get back in bed, eat some of this toast. It should help soak up some of that alcohol."

I did as I was told. I couldn't bear to stand up, anyway. Michael laughed at my paranoia and fed me the eggs and sausage he'd cooked.

———

"Tina, I was so embarrassed," I explained over the phone.

"What kind of drink was that?" Tina asked.

"The damn thing had fire floating on top of it. I should have known better," I said.

"Well, thank God he didn't try anything. He probably would have killed your ass," Tina said.

"No bullshit," I agreed. "I still can't figure out how I managed to put on those clothes. He said I went into the bathroom and everything."

"Shit, ya ass wasn't that drunk. You was sober enough to know you still had a dick," Tina said, laughing.

"I guess I was."

"So, is he your new dude?" Tina asked.

"He proved himself thus far. I just have to see what his bank account looks like," I said.

"Well, make sure you take precautions," Tina slid in. "Please, Tina, not today. I don't feel like the get-out-of-the-game speech," I said.

"Just probe him a little. Shit, he might be gay his damn self. Then you would have a winner," she said.

Truth be told, I'd only been talking to Michael for a week and I was starting to catch feelings for him. I even invited him to Albany for Tina's wedding. We made plans to go to the King of

Prussia Mall and buy something to wear together. This was the test, I figured. I was on my way to the mall to meet Michael with not a dime in my pocket. I would really be able to tell if he was right for me if he splurged on me even though we hadn't had sex yet.

"Hey, baby," I said as I kissed Michael on his cheek. He was standing outside of Neiman Marcus as planned. He was dressed in a pair of jeans with the faded look and a black collar shirt. He had on some black Prada sneakers. He looked regular.

"Were you waiting long?" I asked as we entered the department store.

"About ten minutes," he said.

"The traffic on 76 was jammed," I offered as explanation.

"It's cool," he said as he kissed me on the top of my head.

We walked through Neiman's trying to figure out what we wanted to wear to the wedding. We were trying to coordinate since he was going to be my date. Once we agreed on a color we went our separate ways. We decided to meet in the accessories area in an hour. I tried on so many dresses and skirts and nothing appealed to me. Finally I found the perfect linen dress, a sexy number by Diesel. It was pastel blue and fit to my body just right. It tied behind my neck and flared from the waist down, reminding me of the famous white dress Marilyn Monroe was wearing in a popular photograph of her holding it down.

"Is that what you want?" Michael asked as we were approaching the cash register.

"Yes, it's the only dress in here that fits me perfect," I affirmed.

Michael pulled out his credit card. He didn't have anything to buy for himself, so I could only assume he was planning on paying for my items. I watched him in silence. The cashier placed the dress in a garment bag and the silver Manolo Blahnik stilettos I'd also chosen in a shopping bag. When she gave him the total he handed the woman his platinum Visa. He's the one, I thought to myself.

Michael didn't find anything in the tons of stores we went in, so he wound up buying an off-white linen shirt and pants set from Vizuri on South Street.

We packed up our bags and were headed to New York on a Thursday evening. It was cloudy and drizzling when Michael picked me up from my house. We drove to Thirtieth Street train station to get the seven forty-five departure to Penn Station.

It was a comfortable train ride. I spent most of it cuddled up with Michael. We arrived in Manhattan at nine fifty-two. We were both starving, so immediately after checking into our hotel we ordered room service. Michael came out of his work clothes and lounged around in his boxers, a wife beater, and some sweat socks. I changed into some pajamas from the Victoria's Secret sporty collection. We ate so much and were so tired that we went right to sleep without having sex. I knew that it would only be a matter of time before Michael would ask for some. I was just waiting for that time to come.

———

"CELESS, I am so nervous. I don't believe I'm about to give some-body the rest of my life," Tina said in my cell phone.

Michael and I were on the road, driving to Albany. We had rented a car on Friday. Tina had called me and asked that I talk to her for the entire ride. She was in her own suite alone getting ready for her wedding ceremony.

"Celess, what if I trip down the aisle or what if the minister says my real name because I had to give up my real name for the paperwork, but I did tell him that I wanted to be called Tina, so..."

"Tina, Tina, Tina, calm down. You're just excited. Everything is going to go just right." I tried to settle her. "How far away are y'all?" she asked for the fiftieth time.

"We just passed a sign that said we are seven miles away," I said.

"As soon as y'all get here, come straight to my suite. I need you, girl," Tina said.

Michael waited in the lobby while I went to Tina's rescue. Tina was sitting in a chair looking out the window when I entered her suite.

"Celess!" she squealed, holding her arms out to hug me. Tina sounded like a little girl.

"Hey, girl," I said, hugging her tight.

Tina stood up and walked over to the dresser. "I'm so glad you could be here for this, Celess," she said, glancing up at me as she rummaged through the top drawer.

She retrieved a small box from the drawer and handed it to me. "Celess, I want you to have this. Even though you are not in the wedding, I want you to wear this today so we'll both have one on."

I took the diamond choker from the box. There was a big heart-shaped diamond dangling from it that had to be at least five carats alone. On the back of the heart it read, "Forever My Friend." It was beautiful. I had never owned so many diamonds on one item before in my life. "This is beautiful," I gasped. Tears were forming in my eyes.

"Don't start crying, 'cause you gonna make me cry and it took too long to put on this makeup," Tina said. It was five-thirty. The wedding was scheduled for six. I helped Tina get into her gown. She looked amazing. It was a straight, form-fitting gown that brushed her ankles. It was white, of course, with diamonds embroidered on and around the bust-line and on the spaghetti straps. It was very simple but very pretty. She wore a simple slide with a diamond-covered strap across the toes and a small stiletto heel. She carried a single white rose. Her hair was pulled up into a bun and she wore a Chinese bang that was cut neatly and even just over her eyebrows. Her veil was lined with jewels that matched the ones in her dress and shoes. Everything was custom-made with real diamonds. I took plenty of pictures, touched her up, and left her alone so that I could be on my way to the ceremony. It was a little after six. Michael and I were at the park where the wedding was to take place. Derrek was already there, patiently waiting for his bride to arrive. Terry was there with a new woman on his arm. No wonder Tina had sent me two train tickets, I thought. "Hello, Celess," Terry said as he took his seat beside me. "Beautiful day out, hahn?"

"Yeah, very nice," I said. "Oh, Terry, this is Michael. Michael, this is Terry, my brother-in-law-to-be."

The two men reached over me and shook hands. Terry finally decided to introduce his date. "And guys, this is my lovely girl-friend, Princess. Princess, Celess and Michael."

She looked really nice and she had a pretty face, but I knew she was a man. It was just one of those things you could sense. Plus, her name was Princess. Only pets, drag queens, and strippers had names like that. "Nice to meet you, Princess," I said with a fake smile.

For some reason, I was jealous. I didn't know why, considering I really didn't like Terry and I had somebody who looked three times better than him anyway. It was a total of fifteen people present for Tina and Derrek's wedding—small and private just like they wanted it. There was no bridal party. There wasn't even a best man or a bridesmaid. But that's how Tina wanted it to be. Her exact words were, "No offense, but I want the emphasis to be on me and my husband and nobody else." I respected that.

The ceremony lasted about a half hour and it went smoothly. Tina was so happy. I could see it all in her face. Derrek was her dream come true and she was his. The two of them were like little lovebirds. Everybody danced and mingled at the reception—all fifteen of us. Michael and I had fun.

"He's nice," Tina said, commenting on Michael. "He's not who I'd expect to see you with, but he's all right."

"I know. I said the same thing," I agreed.

"Well, have fun with him and be careful," Tina said. "I will, I will. You don't worry about me, you go and enjoy your honeymoon," I said.

"Oh, I sure will. Hawaii, Brazil, and Italy? I'm not going to know what to do with myself for these next thirty days!" Tina exclaimed.

I gave her a big hug and saw her onto the helicopter that had come to whisk the newlyweds off to the airport. I slid Tina an envelope with her wedding gift in it. Inside was $3,000 in cashier's checks. It was the last little bit of my diminishing stash. I knew she didn't need the money. She had just married a multi-millionaire. But I figured she could put it up. Rainy days do come up, even for wives of rich men.

SEPTEMBER

"So why don't you show me some of that yoga?" Michael said out of the blue.

I put my soda down on the ceramic table. "What yoga?"

Michael nudged my shoulder, trying to get me off the sofa. "The yoga you teach to your classes," he reminded me. "Come on, don't be shy."

"Baby, we're in the middle of watching a good movie. I'm not doing yoga right now," I whined.

"Since when did *Cops* go from a TV show to a good movie?"

"Well, we're eating popcorn and drinking Cokes, so..."

"So anytime you eat popcorn and drink Coke you're watching a good movie?" he asked.

"It feels that way to me," I answered.

I never should have told him I was a yoga instructor, I thought.

"Whatever," he said. "Come on, show me some moves. I want to do yoga."

"All right!" I finally gave in. I figured I could fake him out with a few things I had learned from class. I moved from Michael's cozy, fluffy couch onto the hardwood floor. I opened my legs to stretch a little.

Thank God I was wearing sweatpants. I was bending forward, allowing my nose to touch the floor.

"First it's important to stretch your muscles," I said with my head facing the floor.

"Is that right?" Michael asked as he crept up behind me, placing my small waist between his thighs.

I sat up and closed my legs abruptly. "You're not watching me," I protested.

"I am watching you," Michael said as he nibbled on my ear.

Michael's hands found their way from my waist to my thighs. He was caressing me and it felt good, but I had to stop him.

"Hands to yourself," I whispered, placing Michael's hands on the floor.

I wanted the same thing Michael wanted at that time, but I just wanted it to be on my terms, not his. I had to be the one in charge, or else he would have a chance to learn all about me. I stood up. Michael grabbed on to my calves while he remained seated on the floor.

"What's wrong?" he asked.

"Nothing, nothing at all. Just let me freshen up," I said as I walked toward the spiral staircase.

I went into the bathroom and changed into some lingerie I had in my overnight bag. It was a Victoria's Secret satin pink and black bra-and-panty set that had a little flirty skirt attached. Beneath the skirt was a package taped in so tight it was almost invisible. Perfect, I thought. I slid my feet into my black feathered high-heeled slippers, took some deep breaths, and looked at myself in the mirror one last time before heading back downstairs to Michael and putting my life on the line. I wasn't sure why I was so nervous about having sex with Michael. I had risked my life with much more dangerous guys than him.

"Whoa!" Michael blurted as I walked down the stairs.

He had some slow music playing and the lights were dim. He was still fully clothed and had sat back down on the floor. I got on my knees and crawled over to him. He reached his arms out to grab me, but I moved them to his side and gently pushed him back onto the floor. I began to unbutton his pants and caress his manhood at the same time. He was aroused. He lifted his head slightly to peek at me while I performed oral sex. When he put his hand on top of my head to control my movements, I kindly removed it and placed it back on the floor. I wanted him to know I was in charge.

Michael had gotten nice and hard and was ready for the real deal. He got up from the floor and repositioned himself on the couch. He came out of all his clothes, throwing each article in a different direction. Then he motioned for me to do the same. I kicked off the slippers and removed my bra, leaving me in nothing but the skirt.

"Take that off too," Michael said as he stared me up and down while stroking his penis.

I ignored him as I slowly approached and placed his hands on my breasts.

I jammed my tongue in Michael's mouth, forcing him to take his mind off of the idea of seeing me completely naked.

"I want you," Michael moaned.

"I want you too," I moaned back.

"Then take me," he said as he quickly slid his erect penis toward my middle.

I jumped back just in time. "Michael," I cautioned with a frown.

My heart was beating a mile a minute. I was having second thoughts about even continuing.

Michael sat up on the couch. "Come here, don't back away

from me," he said, reaching for my hand. "Let me handle this, okay?" I instructed as I backed away from him.

"All right, you got it, but I want to see that coochie," Michael said. "Show me that thing!" he insisted.

I didn't know what Michael was up to. I kept asking myself why was he so adamant about seeing what was in my panties. Usually guys just went with the flow, especially the first time around. Some head and a dominating woman were enough to keep them content. I had to come up with something, and I had to come up with it fast.

"Michael, I'm a virgin," I said.

Michael laughed and replied, "Come on, Celess, stop playing."

"I don't believe in sex before marriage," I continued. "Are you serious?" he asked with a serious face. "Yes," I insisted, "and I can't believe that a man like you don't respect that."

Michael sucked his teeth in disbelief. He looked away from me and reached for his boxers on the far end of the couch. I walked slowly toward him and grabbed his arm, gently pushing him away from his boxers.

I leaned over him and whispered in his ear, "But I hope you don't think I got you all hot and steamy for nothing."

I began to stroke his dick, bringing it back to life. It had gone down once Michael heard the word *virgin*. Michael just sat there, seemingly holding back. He sure wasn't as aggressive as he had been. As I felt his penis rising, I started sucking it, slowly and passionately. Michael began to relax as he leaned his head back against the sofa. He had learned that it was best to let me run the show, as he kept his hands by his sides and gave me full clearance to do what I wanted to do.

I began to slide Michael's slobbered-down dick up and down between my breasts. He was slowly getting back into it as he started pumping his waist up and down. I released Michael's dick as it stood hard and tall.

"What now?" he asked, breathing heavily.

"You just wait there and let me lead the way," I said as I turned out the lights completely.

It's showtime, I thought. While walking back to Michael, I reached in the back of my panties and removed the tape. I quickly grabbed my package and brought it forward. I cuffed my balls and penis and held them in place, keeping them as close to the front as I possibly could. Michael could hardly see me, but just to make sense of things for him, I told him I was playing with myself. He was turned on and was so hard I don't think he gave a shit what I told him. I systematically positioned myself on his lap while holding on to my privates for dear life. My heart was pounding and Michael could tell.

"Celess, are you sure you want to do this? I mean, if you want to hold out..." Michael whispered.

"Anal sex is okay, Michael. As long as my hy—you know, don't get busted," I said. I'd forgotten the name of the thing, or perhaps I never knew it—shit, I wasn't a woman for real. But he knew what I was referring to.

"You don't mind?" Michael asked. "Because I want you to be ready."

"Shh," I whispered. Then with my one free hand I slid his erect penis in my asshole.

"Just let me handle this. Keep your hands to yourself and no sudden movements," I moaned.

"Whatever you say," Michael moaned back.

I felt him quiver as I moved my body up and down on top of his. I got him. It hadn't been easy, but I got him. Michael and I finally had our moment, and I must say it was the most amazing sex I ever had. It was passionate and pleasurable. Granted, I didn't have multiple orgasms like I had with James, but one was enough with Michael.

"Surprise!" Michael shouted.

I opened my eyes and took a couple steps back. I looked up at the vacant building and read the sign. Less is Best Beauty Salon, it read. I was confused at first, but then it clicked—"Less" is me. This was my shop.

"Oh, my God, baby, you didn't!" I yelled.

"Well, you said you wanted your own hair salon," Michael said, smiling.

I jumped in Michael's arms and hugged him tight. I was kissing him on his neck and cheek and lips uncontrollably.

He put me down and said, "Come on, let me show you the inside."

He led me into the place. It was something out of a magazine.

"I designed it especially for you," he said. "I incorporated a little bit of everything you like: the spiral staircase, the long mirrors, the hardwood floors, the built-in shelves, and the archway. Upstairs is a small flat. It has an eat-in kitchen and a lounge area."

Michael paused and searched my face. "Do you like it?"

"Like it? Michael, I love it!" I cried, with my hands over my mouth.

My eyes were watering. I could not believe Michael did this for me.

"How did you do this? I mean, how did you find the time? Oh, my God, Michael, I'm speechless!"

"You know, it was funny, because I had been working on this place before you and I met," Michael began as he took a seat in one of the styling chairs. "By the time we got together, only the cosmetics had to be done. And when you told me that it was your dream to open your own hair salon one day, I got a thought in my head. But of course I had to wait and see where we were headed, you know. The owner planned on selling it once it was finished, so after thinking long and hard, I took it off his hands," Michael explained.

I shook my head, still holding my hands over my mouth.

"Once I paid him for it," Michael continued, "I hired a group of guys to finish it up. We've been working on this day and night."

"Baby, this is...I can't even explain it. Words can't say," I said, wiping my eyes.

Weeks flew by. It had seemed like I would go to sleep on a Monday and wake up on a Friday. But I had no complaints, as all of my days had been filled with bliss. Michael was like a dream come true. I'd grown to love him, and with all that he'd done for me, how could that be a surprise? For the first time in years I had only been dealing with one dude. I was trying to take Tina's advice and slow down. As far as my bills, I had found three stylists and a manicurist. The $2,800 they brought in each month helped out a lot.

I was home alone one day. Michael was in Pittsburgh working. After cooking myself some dinner, I made chicken Alfredo, a salad, and some Pillsbury breadsticks. Thank God for the Foreman grill. It tasted damn near better than a restaurant's. It filled me up too. I was sitting on the couch staring at the Guide Channel trying to find something good to watch. It was a Sunday, so I was bound to find something good on Lifetime.

Ring! Ring!

"Hello."

"Hey, Celess," Tina squealed.

I hadn't spoken to Tina since last month at her wedding.

"Hey, Tina! What's up, girl? How is the honeymoon going?"

"Oh, it's beautiful, girl. We're in Italy now visiting Derrek's family," Tina said.

"Damn, it must be nice," I said.

"It is. And Brazil was nice too. But girl, ain't nothing like

Hawaii. It is so pretty out there. The sun, the water, the people, everything is pretty. Shit, even Michael would be pretty out there," Tina joked.

I just laughed.

"Speaking of Mr. Tall, Dark, and Not-so-Handsome, how is that coming along?"

"Let me see," I teased. "He opened me a salon," I bragged.

"A bar?" Tina asked, disgusted. "A salon, not a saloon."

"A hair salon?" Tina screamed. "Yeah!"

"Get the fuck outta here, you sprung 'im up like that?" Tina joked.

"I know right," I continued to brag.

"So what else been up, miss?" Tina asked.

"Ain't shit. I'm tryna decide if I'm gonna go to Power House on my lonesome," I said with a playful attitude, wanting Tina to regret leaving me.

"Damn, that's right. That concert is coming up, ain't it?" Tina thought aloud.

Right then my other line started beeping. I was waiting for a call from Michael, otherwise I would not have answered it.

"Tina, hold on right quick. That's probably my boo right now. Don't hang up."

"Hello."

"Yeah, can I speak to Celess?"

The voice on the other line was deep but it did not belong to Michael.

"This is she, who is this?" I asked.

"Tariq. Do you remember me?" he asked with an attitude.

I rolled my eyes and returned the attitude. "Yes, Tariq, what is it? I have a call on the other line, long-distance." "This'll only take a minute, trust me. I think you need to get tested for HIV."

"What are you talking about, Tariq? I mean, really, I have

somebody on my other line," I said, totally oblivious to what he said.

"I was tested positive for HIV, Celess, and it's only fair that I make the necessary calls to the people I may have infected." He paused. "Or may have infected me." I held the phone to my ear but said nothing. I didn't click back over to Tina. I didn't want to burden her with some bullshit while she was on her honeymoon. I didn't even respond to Tariq. I just sat there in dead silence, holding the phone to my ear. I heard Tariq saying hello. I even heard the dial tone that phones make when they are off the hook. But I still held the phone to my ear waiting—waiting for a voice to yell, "Wake up."

"Beverly Hill." The nurse called out the false name I gave her.

I stood up after first hesitating and followed the nurse through the door.

"Have a seat," she said.

I sat in the chair that was placed against a wall. I looked around the small room. There were needles, plastic gloves, containers, and charts scattered about. There were brochures and posters on the walls warning people of HIV and AIDS. Chills went up my spine just from reading the information.

"Roll up your sleeve, please," she said as she dampened a cotton ball with alcohol.

I began to do as I was told. I took off my jean jacket and placed it in my lap. Then I proceeded to unbutton the cuff on my blouse. I looked very plain that day. I was not flashy at all. I had my reasons, though. I was feeling down for one, and for two I was trying to be as incognito as possible.

"Understand that if the results of this test come back negative, we still recommend you get another test six months from now. This test will only show results as of six months ago, which means that if you've come in contact with the virus within the past six months it won't show up in this test," the nurse said as she dabbed my arm with the cotton ball.

"Whatever," I mumbled.

I didn't have an attitude. It was just that I was deep in thought. I kept thinking about all of my risky behavior and how that might wind up ending my life. My only worry had been dudes finding out I was a gay man. Never did I worry about getting AIDS, even though it was common among gay guys. But all the dudes I messed with were straight—well, most of them. Plus they were all clean and getting money. They weren't scrub-ass corner boys who put their dick in everything. But come to think about it, that damn O had bitches around every corner and it's no telling how many men he might have had. Shit, he was bound to have one dirty dick.

"You know, AIDS is not a death sentence," the nurse said as she tapped my arm in search of a vein. "Many people are unedu-cated about it and therefore they're scared of it. They're scared to get tested and so they spread it—not intentionally, though, but they do it unaware that they even have it. That's why, believe it or not, you taking the first step and getting tested is a good thing. It's the best thing."

"Ouch," I said as she stuck me with the needle.

I had my face frowned up from the pain as I was looking at my blood fill the needle. The nurse removed the needle, stored the blood, and wiped my arm with an alcohol pad. She then placed a cotton ball over the tiny needle mark and taped it to my arm.

The whole time I sat silently thinking about Michael. What if I'd fucked around and given him some hot shit? It's one thing for a trifling nigga to give it to me, but it's a whole other story for *me* to give it to somebody, especially somebody like Michael. After all he'd done for my trifling ass, I thought.

"Make an appointment to come in for your test results in two weeks, okay?" the nurse instructed me, interrupting my thoughts.

"Yes."

"Have a good one," she said.

As I was leaving the clinic I noticed everybody looking at me with shame. It was as if they knew something I didn't. They looked like they pitied me. The truth was I pitied them for having to live in a world with people like me.

OCTOBER

"Say HO-OH! HO-OH! Say HO-HO! HO-HO!" the loud echo sounded.

Power House was the perfect place to celebrate my clearance. My test had come back negative and I wasn't worried about that six-months shit because I hadn't fucked Tariq within the past six months, so I figured I was cool. I was backstage getting nice off of Alizé red. I was sitting alone in a room with like a thousand groupies, some lucky fans, and a few lingering security guards. My eyes were burning from the thick weed smoke that filled the air. Rappers and members of their entourages would pass by occasionally and peep in. The groupies would go crazy, and it never failed that at least one would get gripped up by a big three-hundred-pound guard and get thrown out the door. I just kept my cool. I wasn't after the rappers or their homies, anyway. I was after the promoters. Promoters were easier to get to and played fewer games. Tina taught me that it was the promoters who paid the entertainers, so if anybody was holding, it was them. Plus, rappers' heads were too swelled, so they liked to take girls on joyrides, and a lot of times girls ended up fucking for nothing except bragging rights. Not me.

"Where's the bathroom?" I asked the big guard at the doorway.

"Right down the hall on your left," he said, pointing in the direction.

I went into the bathroom to check my makeup. I was okay, but I needed to re-up on my lipstick courtesy of the numerous cups of Alizé. I figured I would linger in the bathroom for a while until it was time to make a move.

Close to the end of the show, right before people flooded the hall, I approached this dude who was walking past me. His eyes were glued to mine even though he walked by swiftly.

"Excuse me." I hollered out. "Where is the exit?" I asked as if I was lost.

"This way. Why?" he said, looking back at me. "Well, if you lead, can I follow?" I asked.

"I'm not going to the exit yet, sweetheart," he said hurriedly.

"I didn't say you were," I said, walking toward him. "Go 'head," I said. "I can keep up."

The guy raised his eyebrows and looked at the guy who was with him. I could tell neither of them was used to somebody like me coming at them, because I took them by surprise.

"I'm not no star, sweetheart," the guy said with a chuckle.

"I can make you one," I said, smiling.

"As flattered as I am, I have to turn down your offer. I'm in a rush," he said as he started to walk away.

I heard the other guy mumble, "I don't believe you turned that away."

So I commented, "Some people *already* have it all." The guy stopped walking and turned back to face me. He shook his head. "You're hurting me, sweetheart.

Got damn, you are."

"Just tell me when and where to meet you," I said. "Two at Four Seasons, suite twenty sixteen."

I smiled and watched him and the other guy continue their brisk walk to the end of the hall. I wasn't one hundred percent sure he was a promoter, but he was somebody, and my instincts were telling me to ride. I went to the South Street Diner to pass time. I ordered the hungry woman breakfast and pigged out. It was packed. I was alone. I was thinking about Michael and how I would much rather have been with him that night, cuddling and making love, watching a few flicks, and maybe playing a game of Scrabble. Yeah, I guess I was falling in love. But I was missing the other stuff that I had been faithful to for four years—the different ballers, the one-night stands, the money, the flash, the fun, the rush. I wanted it bad. And this was the perfect opportunity to get it back, while Michael was away working on a contract.

It was two-eleven when I knocked on suite 2016. There was no answer. At first I was thinking the dude had played me and fed me some bullshit. But I waited around for a little while, hoping he didn't. It was two thirty-eight when I finally decided to leave. I walked toward the elevator.

"Where you goin'?"

I turned around and saw the guy placing the key in the door. I was relieved, but I had to let him know that I was pissed. I looked at my watch.

"Two o'clock was a half hour ago," I said.

He smiled and said, "Right, so we definitely don't have any more time to waste, do we?"

I grinned and followed him into his suite. It was big and nicely designed, but I'd seen better. Besides, he had it looking like a pigsty.

"I never did get your name," he said as he started throwing things from the bed onto the floor.

"Ce...lina," I said, deciding at the last minute not to give my name.

"Selena?" he asked. "Like the singer?"

"Yes, like the singer," I said, standing in the same position as if I was on my pivot.

"Come in, have a seat. You have to excuse this mess, I was rushing for the show."

"What's your name?" I asked as I walked over to the bed.

"Mann," he answered.

I sat down and he sat next to me. He was an old head, probably in his mid-to late thirties. He was short and somewhat stocky, with a cute light brown face: squinted eyes, a pointed nose, and thin lips. He had a nicely groomed mustache and goatee and a low cut that revealed a nice grade of waves. He admired me, I could tell.

"You are very attractive, you know that?" he said. "And you look good as hell in that dress. Is that a dress?" he asked, placing his hand on my thigh.

I was wearing a Missoni minidress. It was colorful, with blotches of aqua and hot pink, and it came to the middle of my thighs. It had long, loose sleeves that gathered at the wrists, giving it a balloon effect. My legs were bare and I wore a pair of Marc Jacobs leather hot pink pointy-toe pumps with a kitten heel. I wore my hair in a weave that was parted in the middle with loose curls at the tips that fell a little past my shoulders. My makeup was soft but vibrant, with one coat of hot pink on my eyelids and lips and a small amount of pink blush. I had on diamond hoops and a diamond Rolex, and I carried a small hot pink leather clutch. I wore no coat despite the fact it was the end of October.

"You look like something out of magazine," Mann said, rubbing my thigh.

I rolled my eyes and said, "Enough about me. I want to know about you. What are you into?"

"Well, I told you earlier I'm not no star, you know. I'm just a regular cat doing regular things." He was beating around the bush.

"A presidential suite in the Four Seasons is not regular in any sense of the word," I said. "Come on, tell me what you do. You run the show, don't you? You're that man behind the scenes that nobody knows but who got the big bank, ain't you?" I asked him in between nibbling on his ear.

He smiled. "I don't know about the big bank, but I am behind the scenes. I'm a promoter-slash-manager. So, yes, I am the one who runs the show."

"See, now, was that hard?" I asked, fondling him. "And what about you? What do you do, because usually the gold diggers go after the performers, the ones who show their hands. I never in all my years in this business had one come after me. Shit, they even go after the bodyguards and the drivers. But they never come after me. So what are you into?"

I smiled at him. "Why dig for gold when diamonds play the surface? I'm a professional."

"I see," Mann said, as he lay on his back and closed his eyes.

NOVEMBER

"**G**ood morning, yall," I said as I walked into the salon. I got the usual "Hey, girl, what's up? You look tired." I sat down at the receptionist's desk and pulled out my bacon, egg, and cheese on a hoagie roll. I took two bites out of it and was interrupted by a phone call on my cell.

"Yes," I answered, frustrated.

"Put that sandwich down and have brunch with me." The voice on the other end sounded so clear, as if it were right next to me.

"Ba-by!" I squealed as I jumped out of my seat.

Michael was walking toward me from the back of the salon.

"Y'all knew my baby was back and y'all didn't say nothing," I teased.

It had been a whole month since I'd seen Michael, and I missed the hell out of him.

"Oooh maaa!" He gave me a big kiss on my forehead and squeezed me in his muscular arms.

"When did you get back?" I asked, sounding like a little girl.

"Late last night. I didn't want to call because I figured you were asleep."

"So, where are we doing brunch?" I asked excitedly. "Somewhere nice," Michael said as he tossed my keys to Kelly, the first stylist.

"Here, you lock up tonight. We won't be back in time to close," he told Kelly.

I grabbed my black and white graffiti Louis Vuitton bag off the counter and followed Michael out the door. We got in his white-on-white S500 and sped off. We hit 676 and I put my seat back and fell asleep. When I woke up we were on 495 south headed to Maryland.

"The harbor?" I asked in amazement.

"Yeah, there's a nice breakfast spot down here I've been wanting to take you."

Michael maneuvered the Benz S-class into a parking spot. I checked my appearance in the mirror and we hopped out. It was nice outside for a November day. The sun was shining bright and the air was thin but crisp, creating a light, comfortable breeze. I had on a pair of low-rider straight-leg jeans that were smack tight. The black cashmere leg warmers on top of them fell right over the top of my black leather pointy-toe stiletto boots. I had on a black cashmere fitted hooded sweater that revealed a little of my stomach underneath a white fitted waist-length leather jacket by Kenneth Cole. I looked cute and casual, very much dressed for the occasion, fortunately.

"Two?" the hostess asked.

"Yes, nonsmoking, please," Michael said. "Right this way."

We followed the hostess through a half-empty diner. She led us to a booth, handed us two menus, and told us our waitress would be with us shortly.

"This is a nice place," I said as I examined the decor.

"Yeah, I used to come out here every Saturday when I lived out Silver Spring," Michael said.

"You lived everywhere."

"Well, when I get a contract that takes one or more years, I have no choice, right?"

Michael and I ate a delicious breakfast and enjoyed each other's company. We walked along the harbor hand in hand and he told me all about the building he just finished in Pittsburgh. He made $75,000 off that job alone. His bank account had to be O'ed up. Anytime he was able to open me a salon in Northern Liberties, pay rent on Delaware Avenue, and afford month-long hotel stays every now and then, he was paid.

Michael and I spent the whole day in Baltimore. We did some shopping while we were at the harbor. I spent like $2,000 (of Michael's money) in Victoria's Secret buying up just about everything from their new collection. Then we drove to a movie theater on Eastern Boulevard to see *Minority Report.* After the movie, Michael took me to this restaurant called Cactus Willies. That had to be the best buffet spot I've ever been to. Michael dropped me off at my car at a quarter to ten. The salon was closed up. The cold dark streets were empty. I would have spent the night with him, but he was exhausted and just needed to be alone in his own house in his own bed. I respected that.

When I walked in the door, I noticed I had messages. I plopped down on my couch and pressed the button to listen.

"Hey, Selena, what's up? It's Mann. Give me a call, all right? Peace."

My man is back now, I have no need for you, I thought.

The next message was from Tina. "Celess, girl, you have to call me! You won't believe who I saw down here!"

I picked up the phone to call her. I hadn't spoken to her in a while, anyway, and I needed to update her, especially about Tariq giving me that AIDS scare.

"Hi, Derrek, is Tina there?"

"Hey, Celess, honey, how've you been, darling?" "Oh, just fine, thanks for asking. How about yourself? I heard the honeymoon was nice," I said.

"It was magnificent, thanks. But hold on, here she is." "Hello," Tina said.

"What's up, girl?"

"What's up?"

"I got your message."

"Oh, Celess!" Tina said. "I saw James yesterday!" "For real? Where?"

"Me and Derrek had floor seats to the Lakers versus the Rockets. Why was this nigga standing right near us while he was waiting to substitute some dude? He looked me right in the eye and gave an ice grill out this world. I just smiled. Derrek was like, what was that about? I was like, I used to tease the hell out of his nerd-ass in school."

"For real," I said. "So, he's still pissed off, hahn?" "Girl, *pissed* ain't the word. If looks could kill, y'all would be planning my funeral right now."

"Well, I'm over that. I took your advice. I slowed down a lot. I just fuck with Michael right now and I strap up with him, especially after Tariq called me with the bullshit he called me with."

"What bullshit did Tariq call you with?" "This nigga got HIV, Tina."

"What? Well, what about you, are you straight?" "I'm cool," I said.

"You went and got tested?" "Yeah."

"Well, when did he tell you this? I mean, why are you just now tellin' me? I would've flew up there and went to the doctors with you," Tina insisted.

"I know, but it's cool. You were in Italy with Derrek. Plus I wasn't about to have you worrying about me on ya honeymoon, you know?"

Tina exhaled. "That's crazy," she said. "That's why I'm glad I'm out. I'm glad I'm done. That game will swallow you up."

"No bullshit," I agreed.

Tina quickly changed the subject. "So, the last time we spoke, you were debating whether or not you were going to go to Power House by yourself. Did you go?" "Yeah. And I met this guy named Mann, a promoter."

"You fucked him?" Tina butted in.

"Tina," I whined, "I was lonely and I needed that G." "A measly G? The last I checked, you had a nigga buying you hair salons. What do you mean, you needed that G?"

"I still got my other needs. Tina, come on, don't act like you don't know. Shit, I need more than my bills paid. I need my image maintained, and Premarin and electrolysis never been cheap. What am I supposed to do, stop taking my hormones and grow a beard? I don't think so." "Celess, but you gotta stop getting those needs met like that. You're already pressing your luck with
Michael."

"How?"

"He doesn't know you are a man, Celess, that's how!" "Just like Khalil, Drake, Jahuan, et cetera, et cetera, didn't know you were a man!"

"Right! And I could have got my ass killed!"

"So you're telling me that if you never found Derrek and never got married, you would have still got out the game?"

"I don't know, Celess. It was Derrek who made me even think about the shit I was doing. So, honestly, probably not. If I never met Derrek I would not have even thought about getting out the game, but I did. And everything happens for a reason."

"Well, my reason didn't come to me yet. What am I supposed to do?"

"Celess, tell Michael. He's a nice guy and he loves you. He might not mind. I have ideas about him, anyway. He might be gay or he might be bi. Just tell him," Tina pleaded. "Before it's too late."

What Tina said about Michael weighed heavily on my mind for days. Every time I saw him I wanted to tell him. I didn't know if it was all in my mind or not, but it did seem like Michael could have been gay. The way he dressed was clue number one. But he wasn't feminine. It was little things like his neatness and his emphasis on personal hygiene. I didn't know. Maybe I just wanted him to be gay so that I could tell him about me and we could go on and have what Tina and Derrek had. That would have been the only way I would have satisfied Tina and left the game for good, even if Michael can't give me all the things I was used to. I could learn to be content with the life he was capable of giving me.

"Damn, what did I do to deserve this?" Michael asked as he walked into my dining room.

"What haven't you done?" I said as I pulled the chair out for him to sit down.

Michael was pleased with the surprise candlelit dinner I had prepared for him. He was smiling and didn't look ready to stop.

I took his coat for him and laid it on the couch. He had on a pair of carpenter jeans and a white long john shirt. After all, he did just think he was coming over to dig my car out of the snow.

"For somebody who spent a whole day cooking, you sure look good," he said, referring to my red leather Bebe pants and my red bustier-like blouse. "Are you sure you slaved over a hot stove, or is this takeout?" he teased.

"Just because you never seen a cook look as good as me does not mean it ain't possible," I shot back.

I served Michael his spaghetti and meatballs and his side salad. I poured him a glass of hot apple cider. I buttered his dinner rolls, and then I sat across from him. The table was set perfect and I had Sade playing softly from the stereo in the living room. The mood was just right. "Um, this is pretty good," Michael said, complimenting me on my meal.

"I'm glad you like it. I put my foot in this."

"Well, it tastes like you put your butt in it too, 'cause it's booty-licious," Michael joked.

I just giggled and then started contemplating how I was going to tell him. I had practiced over and over. First, I planned to get on the topic of gay men and see what his reactions would be. Then, if my instincts told me to, I would come out and tell him.

"Next time I'll be expecting you to cook for me," I said.

"That is not a problem, 'cause I can throw down," Michael said, stuffing a forkful of spaghetti in his mouth.

"Is that right?"

"That's right," Michael said with confidence.

"Well, you know what they say about men who can cook?"

"What's that?"

"They're usually fat or gay...and you're not fat," I said, lifting my eyes from my plate and onto him.

He looked up at me and said, "I'm very happy."

I just smiled. I couldn't do it. He didn't give me a readable response. It was then that I knew it would never work between us. There was no way I would be able to keep my secret from him much longer, and without him knowing the truth, I would have to distance myself from him. On that note, I decided to just keep doing what I'd been doing. It was what I knew best, anyway. It was what got me all I had now. I had to withdraw some of my feelings for Michael. I had to go back to my old ways. I had to keep playing.

DECEMBER

"Hap-py birth-day toooo yooou, Hap-py birth-day tooo yooou, Hap-py birth-day dear Celeesss, Hap-py birth-day tooooooo yooooou," Tina sang over the phone.

"Thank you," I said modestly. "And thank you for the picture. It's bangin'."

"You're welcome. I knew you would like it. That was back when it was just you and me runnin' the streets. Did you get that envelope?"

"What envelope, the card?"

"No, the envelope that was in back of the picture. Go look," Tina demanded.

I got up off my bed and walked over to the framed poster-sized painting of Tina and me on my twenty-first birthday a year ago. We were smiling ear to ear, posed up in the Range Rover, holding a bottle of Cristal and a wad of money. It brought back many memories. I turned the picture around and saw a white envelope wrapped in the plastic.

"I see it," I told Tina as I made a hole in the plastic.

"Open it! Hurry up!" Tina said excitedly.

I got the envelope out of the plastic and opened it. Inside was a bunch of papers stapled together and folded. I opened them, and a loose paper fell out into my lap.

I read the letter aloud. " 'Celess, this is the first birthday since we met that you spent without me, and it has made me realize just how much I miss you.'"

I looked at the bundle of papers. Meanwhile, Tina was silent on the other end of the phone.

"A deed?" I asked, confused as hell.

"It's a three-bedroom, two-bath condo, on the hill, fireplace, high ceilings, the works, and it's for you. Happy birthday!"

"Tina, I don't get it," I said, still confused.

"Celess, it's not rocket science! I want you to move down here," Tina snapped.

"What? Move to L.A.? But what am I gonna do down there?" I asked, dumbfounded.

"Don't worry about all that. You're my girl. You know I got you," Tina assured me.

"I know you're well off, but that's for now. It's no guarantee you'll be married to Derrek forever. I mean, he is twice your age. And I don't think it's a good idea for me to depend on his money. Shit, I'm not the nigga's wife," I told her.

"Well, we're gonna ride the bitch till the wheels fall off," Tina said. "And if push comes to shove, we'll go back to runnin' G on niggas for a living."

"Now, that's the Tina I know!" I said, getting all excited.

"So are you coming or what?"

There was a brief silence. I thought about Michael. I was really feeling him, and you could call it love, but I knew the reality of our situation and it was already in my mind that one day our relationship would have to end—one day soon.

"All right," I said.

Tina screamed joyously on the other end of the phone. I was happy too, but I just needed time to take it all in.

Tina and I made plans to bring the New Year in together one last time in Philly where it all began. I was expecting her in two weeks, and we had major plans. In the meantime I had a lot of preparing to do for my new life in L.A. I had to work on selling my house and my car. I had to do something with my furniture. But the most difficult thing I had to do was wrap things up with Michael. I kept trying to pipe myself up. The day would come sooner or later, I told myself. Even if I stayed in Philly, I would not have been able to maintain a relationship with him for but so long.

"L.A.? For what?" Michael asked. "To be with Tina," I said softly.

"Tina's married. She has her husband out there with her. What does she need you there for?"

"You don't understand," I said.

"Well, then, help me understand. I mean, I opened you a hair salon, which I thought was your dream come true, and now after only three months you're ready to just up and abandon it. And what about us? Correct me if I'm wrong, Celess, but I thought we had something good going on."

"We did, we do, but it's just that..." I took a deep breath. "I'm not all what I'm cracked up to be." I sighed. Michael sat back on the couch and put his hands over his face. He shook his head and then looked at me, confused.

"What are you talking about?" he asked.

"Listen, Michael, I like you a lot. Honestly. I've been with a few dudes and none of them were anything like you. I mean, I don't know how to say this, but I'm used to ballin' dudes who fine as shit and can have any girl they want but still take care of me—"

Michael cut me off. "So what are you saying? You're some type of whore?"

I rolled my eyes. "Yes!" I said, pissed.

Michael was dumbfounded. I caught him off guard. He did not expect that answer. "What?"

"I *was* a whore, okay? I fucked guys for money, cars, clothes, this house! Just like I fucked you for that hair salon!"

Pop! Michael slapped me right across my face. I was stunned. I didn't know whether to hit him back or just tell him to get the fuck out. My instincts told me to go with the latter.

"Get the fuck out of my house," I said, holding my stinging face.

"I'm not going anywhere until you give me a fuckin' explanation! I didn't give you that salon for sex. I gave it to you because I actually cared enough about you to help you achieve your fuckin' goal! You're right, Celess, I'm nothing like the guys you're used to dealing with. I'm not a trick. I don't pay for sex. I was looking for a woman, a relationship, somebody I could share good things with, not some convenient pussy!"

"Well, that's just what I mean, Michael! I'm not that one! I'm not the girl you marry!" I shouted with tears streaming down my face.

"I'm a slut whore with no fuckin' morals or values or feelings! I'm a fuckup! Okay? I'm a fuckup!"

Michael grabbed me and squeezed me in his arms. I started crying heavily, and as much as I should have, I couldn't resist him. I had fallen deep for him. I wanted him more than I knew, but it was no way. It was not possible. I was a man. I could never have what a woman has and that's what Michael wanted so desperately.

"You're not a fuckup. Maybe you just made some mistakes. Okay, I'm sorry. You're sorry. Let's work this out, okay?" Michael asked with cracks in his voice.

He continued, "I was being selfish. When I go out of town on business for months at a time, you understand. I should have been the same way with you, I'm sorry. And I swear to God I am sorry for putting my hands on you. I should have never done that no matter what. No matter how mad you make me, I will never touch you again."

Michael held me in his arms and went on and on. I was still crying and even he started to shed some tears. He really was trying to make it work, and that made it worse for me because I knew it wouldn't.

"Celess, I want to be with you more than anything. I've been looking high and low for a woman like you, and now that I have you I'm not trying to let you go," Michael said.

"Michael," I whimpered, "I'm moving to L.A. I made up my mind. And as bad as I want to be with you, I can't. We'll be too far away. It just wouldn't work."

Michael stepped back and looked into my eyes. His face was damp from his tears. He held my arms down to my sides.

"Look at me, Celess," he said as he placed one of his hands on my chin and gently lifted my face, forcing me to look into his eyes.

"I love you, Celess. I do. I will move to L.A. with you. I want to be with you, Celess, bad. And I won't let you leave me," he said seriously.

I dropped my head and stared down at the floor. My heart was burning. I wanted to scream. I loved this man and he loved me, but despite that, we could never have the meaningful relationship that we both wanted. A million thoughts a minute were running through my mind. I kept hearing Tina's voice saying, "Tell him, he might not mind, tell him." I thought about it. Michael loved me so much that if I did tell him right here and now that I was really a man, gay or not, he probably would still want to be with me. But what if he didn't? What if he snapped? But if he did snap, what was the worst he could do? Leave? That's what I wanted, anyway, so I figured what the hell. I weighed my options. If I tell him and he stays, I'll finally be free, I thought. I will be able to get out of the game for good. If I tell him and he leaves, I can get on that plane in two weeks and start a whole new life in L.A. It seemed like a win-win situation for me.

"Michael, sit down," I said.

I remained standing while Michael sat back down on my couch. I looked at him and he looked at me. He loved me so much I could see it all on his face and it was scary.

"Michael, I really love you. I could marry you today. You are everything I could ever ask for in a man. But I been keeping something from you that I can't keep any longer. And I know that when I tell you, you'll probably leave me alone forever. I know I might lose the only true love I ever had, but I have to tell you because I want to be fair with you and you really deserve better."

I took a deep breath and said, "I'm a...a..." I began to cry before I could get it out.

"I'm a man," I said finally.

"What?"

I stood there crying, waiting for his response. He stood up.

"You're a what? A man?"

I burst into tears and reached out to grab Michael.

He pushed my arms out of his way.

"I don't understand, Celess. What are you telling me?" "Michael, I was born a boy. Technically, I'm a man.

I mean, I'm a woman on the inside, but I have male parts..." I was trying my best to explain.

"Male parts? So you're saying you have a..." Michael said, not able to complete his sentence.

I nodded yes as I sobbed uncontrollably.

"How could you do this to me, Celess? How could you lie to me about some shit like that? Are you crazy?" "Michael, I'm sorry, okay? I'm sorry. It's just that Tina and me, we've been doing this since we were teenagers. I really want to be a woman, I do. It's like

I was born in the wrong body. Everything about me is feminine. Look at me. I work hard at this. I'm a gay man. I don't want to be, but it's who I am. I really wish I could snap my fingers and become a woman, but I can't. I plan on getting the operation, but in time. It's not something that you decide overnight," I cried, trying my best to explain a complicated situation.

Michael stood stiffly as he listened to me. He was taking it all in, every word.

Then his face frowned up and he asked, "Are you saying I slept with a man?"

"I'm sorry, Michael," I whimpered.

"Well, what the hell does that make me? A faggot?" he asked, not looking for an answer.

I kept quiet as I held my hands over my face.

"I can't believe this shit! How?" Michael asked, still in shock.

"Michael, I could have just left and went to L.A. without even telling you," I said, trying to show him that I really did care about him.

"What?" Michael shouted. "So you think you're doing me a favor? You pretend to be a woman for four months, you use me, take my money, you make love to me. You made love to me, what was that, Celess? Huh? How did you make love to me?" Michael asked, looking to me for a response.

"I don't want to go into that right now, Michael, and that's not important, anyway," I told him, not wanting to add fuel to the fire.

"Not important? Are you sick or something? Really, are you mentally ill? You tell me that you are a man with a dick, but how you made love to me is not important. Are you hearing yourself? IT IS IMPORTANT, CELESS!" he screamed.

I could see rage in Michael's eyes as he snatched his coat from off my love seat. He walked past me, disgusted. He did not look at me, but from what I could see, he was crying. On his way out, he picked up a glass vase that sat on a pedestal in the foyer and threw it at the wall. The slam of the door was the last thing I heard. I threw myself on my couch. I clenched my fists and started punching myself on my legs. I was crying uncontrollably. I was hurting.

Tina got to my house three days after Christmas as planned, and for the entire two days that she'd been there, Michael was all I talked about.

"It's not the end of the world, Celess," Tina said. "He hasn't answered any of my calls. I left him message after message. He knows my flight leaves tomorrow and he still won't talk to me."

"You are about to go to L.A. and start a whole new life. It's about time you leave all of this drama behind, anyway," Tina said as she helped me place my clothes in suitcases.

"I just hate that it has to be this way. Why couldn't he have been with it?" I was thinking aloud. Tears began to form.

"Celess, when are you going to let go of the sensitive shit? Damn, you ain't changed a bit," Tina said. "Just be glad all you got was a smack and a broken vase. Shit, it could have been worse."

I sighed. "I know."

"Just cheer up. Tonight we're gonna bring the New Year in right! Just like old times! We're hittin' up every club, every bar, and every party in the city! It's gonna be on and poppin'!" Tina yelled.

I wiped my eyes and smiled. I slapped Tina's hand. I was trying to convince myself that everything was going to be okay, but deep down inside I knew it wasn't.

"That's cute," I told Tina, complimenting her on her fur coat.

It was a sporty baby pink, blue, and white short rabbit with a baby pink ribbed collar and cuffs. She wore a pair of fitted low-rider Diesel jeans and a wife beater. To match her coat she had on a pair of baby pink Manolo Blahnik Tim boots. She looked fly.

"Thank you," Tina said as she whirled around, slowly

modeling the coat. "That jacket is hot too," she said, returning the compliment.

I was in a short black leather Harley-Davidson coat with a fox collar, a pair of Seven jeans, and a red big-neck sheer sweater. I had on some red pointy-toe Prada stilettos and a matching over-sized bag. We both looked sporty but fly.

Tina was in the powder room putting on her final touches, eyelashes, and makeup. I was in the living room moving my luggage to the foyer. Our flight was scheduled to depart from Philadelphia at ten-twenty in the morning, so I wanted to have everything ready and by the door. Especially since we knew we were going to get home drunk as skunks and have no time or balance to do anything in the morning. We already had a town car scheduled to pick us up from my house at eight o'clock and everything.

"I'm ready, you ready?" Tina asked, exiting the powder room.

"Yeah, let me just get my keys and we out," I said, grabbing for the small Gucci key ring that bonded my keys.

Ding-dong!

Tina and I both looked at each other, confused. "Who are you expecting?" Tina asked. "Nobody," I said, just as bewildered as she.

"Who is it?" I asked too lazy to look through the peephole.

"It's me, man, open the door." The masculine voice sounded agitated.

I cracked open the door. "Khalil?" "Celess, where Tina?"

"What are you doing here?" I asked, surprised.

Khalil made his way through my front door. Tina was standing right behind me in the foyer.

"Tina, let me holla at you real quick, over here," Khalil said as he walked into my living room.

Tina looked back at me with a confused expression on her

face. I closed the front door and we followed him into the living room.

"Yo, Celess, can I have a minute with Tina, please?" Khalil asked. "I know y'all all dressed and ready to hit the streets, but I need a minute."

I didn't know about Tina, but I was nervous. Tina gave me a look that told me to wait in the foyer. So I did. But I listened closely to what they were saying.

"When did you get out?" Tina asked curiously.

"Never mind all that. I'm out, that's all that matters," Khalil said.

Tina got to the point. "Okay, well, what's the surprise visit for? I mean, you pop up here at Celess's house after, what, a fuckin' year, and you're coming at me sideways, for what?"

"First of all, lower your fuckin' voice. Second of all, I went past your house and your grandmom told me you was staying with Celess, so that's why I came here to Celess's house."

"Okay, so now that you found me here, what's up?" "You know what the fuck is up. James wrote me a long letter—now you tell me what the fuck is up," Khalil said.

I went back into the living room because at that point I knew exactly what Khalil was there for.

"Matter fact, why don't both of y'all tell me what the fuck is up," Khalil said.

"Listen, neither of us has time for this shit right now. I'm sure you have a lot of people you want to see, being as though you just got released from prison and everything," Tina said sarcastically.

"Naw, I got plenty of time. And I got released almost two months ago, so I made all my visits. Matter fact, I went to see James play in L.A. a couple weeks ago, and it was funny 'cause he told me he seen you, and I was looking for you but I couldn't catch up with you, but I knew I would eventually catch up with you. I made it my business to catch up with you."

Tina rolled her eyes and looked at me. I was standing there contemplating how we should handle the situation. I was ready to go for the phone, but Tina gave me a hint that she had everything under control.

"I don't know what y'all lookin' so lost for, y'all home," Khalil said as he stood up from the sofa.

I took a deep breath. "Khalil, this isn't the time or the place," I said.

"You need to shut the fuck up!" Khalil snapped. "Don't even involve her!" Tina said in my defense. "I didn't involve her, she involved me! Both of y'all bitches involved me!"

Tina started to walk away from Khalil toward the front door. I followed her lead.

"Where the fuck do you think you're going?" Khalil asked as he pushed past me and grabbed Tina's arm. Tina was scared, I could tell, but she played cool.

"Just tell me one thing, Tina," Khalil began. "What's that?" Tina asked, with tears in her eyes and a smile on her face.

"Is what James told me true?"

Tina rolled her eyes and said, "Celess, go wait for me in the car. I'm only gonna be a minute."

"I'm waiting in here," I insisted. Regardless how scared I was, and how bad I would have loved to have waited in the car. I wasn't about to leave Tina in there with Khalil by herself.

"You damn right you're waiting in here," Khalil said as he grabbed my arm with his free hand.

I swung on him and yanked away from him. Tina took advantage of the opportunity and yanked away from him too. We both dashed for the door and then we heard a loud *pop*. Tina fell down on my living room floor. I turned around, and Khalil was pointing a gun at me.

"Tina!" I screamed, startled and frozen.

Tina rolled onto her back. She was bleeding from a small hole in the back of her leg.

"Leave Celess out of this. This is between me and you," she said with tears streaming down her face. That was the first time I actually seen Tina cry.

"You know what, bitch, you fucked with the wrong one! I'm gonna kill you right in front of ya little boyfriend, and then I'm gonna kill him! You played the wrong card this time! You fucked with the wrong one!"

POP! POP!

"TINA! TINA!" I screamed at the top of my lungs. I dropped to the floor and placed my hands over Tina's drooped head, trying to comfort her. My hands were immediately drenched with Tina's blood. I was shaking uncontrollably. I looked up at Khalil one last time.

POP!

My head fell up against the wall. My body was lifeless. My mind went blank.

I woke up to silence. My face felt heavy. I could only see the ceiling. I lifted my arms and felt my face. It was covered with bandages. I panicked. I opened my mouth to speak, but only a whisper came out.

A nurse appeared. "Hi, there," she said in a soft tone. She was smiling. "My name is Nurse Schwartz. I'm going to be taking care of you."

"What the fuck are you smiling about? Where am I? What is all this shit on my face? Where is Tina?"

"Calm down. You lost a lot of blood, honey. We wouldn't want you have a seizure again."

"Seizure? What do you mean, seizure?" I asked. "You keep passing out. You wake up and get yourself all worked up and then you faint. Take deep breaths," she said.

I followed her instructions. I took several deep breaths, but my head was racing and I couldn't help it. I needed to know what was happening.

"All right, I'm calm. Now tell me what's going on." "You were shot with a thirty-eight-caliber shotgun at close range. You are lucky to be alive," she said bluntly.

"Where is Tina?" I asked, not the least bit concerned about myself.

"Is Tina the woman who was with you?"

"Yes, she was just right here. Where is she? I need to talk to her."

"You can't speak to her right now."

"Then when can I speak to her? I need to see her. I need to talk to her. I need to make sure she's all right."

"When you're feeling a little better, okay?"

"I'm feeling better now. I need to see Tina. Where is she?"

The nurse grabbed my hand and held it firmly. "Calm down. We don't want you to pass out. Right now you need to calm down."

"Then tell me where Tina is! I can't calm down! I need to see Tina!"

The nurse swallowed and said, "Tina is not here." "Where is she? I need to talk to her!"

The nurse held my hand tighter. I felt my body beginning to tremble.

"Just tell me where she is!"

"Calm down, please, for your own good."

My body started trembling. I couldn't control it. My hands were shaking. My eyes were rolling in my head. "She's having another one, Doctor!" The nurse's voice called out.

I was having a seizure.

THE AFTERMATH

Four weeks after I was hospitalized, the seizures went away. I could sit up on my own. I could stand for more than six minutes without falling.

I was ready to go home—to my new home.

My house was sold while I was recovering. I used the money to buy another one, a little smaller but in the same neighborhood. I sold my car and the condo that Tina and Derrek had bought for me, so I was sitting on a nice little stash. Plus I had money coming in from the duplex Tariq had bought for me. So my medical bills were paid and I had enough money to live off for a while before I would need to turn to disability.

"Hi, darling," a familiar voice said.

I put my pudding cup down on the tray and turned toward the door of my hospital room.

"Der-rek," I sang.

"Look at you sitting up," Derrek said.

I opened my arms to accept his hug. He pulled away from me and looked me up and down.

"You're looking a lot better these days," he said with tears in his eyes. "How do you feel?"

"I should be asking you that," I said.

Derrek wiped his eyes. "She's at peace, that's for sure," he said, forcing a grin.

I sniffed to keep from crying and said, "I'm so sorry I missed the funeral."

"I know that. But it wasn't safe for you to go, not with your injuries. And Tina would never have wanted you to risk your life to see her in a coffin," he assured me.

"Well, how was it? Tell me every detail," I told him. "Well, let's see, I purchased the land where she and

I got married, and buried her right there. It was a small funeral, smaller than the wedding. The minister said a few words and we all went up one at a time to view the body. The casket was beautiful. It was marble with solid gold trimming. Tina looked beautiful, too. They did her up real well. You would have been happy. She was dressed in her wedding gown with her veil covering her face. You know, to hide the wounds. Her hands were folded together, holding a bouquet of white roses," Tears gathered in Derrek's eyes.

"Forever was too short," I said as I clutched against my chest the diamond choker she had given me to wear at her wedding. My heart was crushed. I broke down into tears. Derrek held me in his arms and we cried together. I could not believe that I would never see Tina again. Every time I thought about it, I prayed for Khalil's death. And my prayers were answered. I got a letter from the police, letting me know Khalil's sentence. One of my neighbors called the cops right after he heard the first shot. See, Khalil thought he would get away with it because it was New Year's Eve. He thought people wouldn't call the cops when they heard the shots simply because that's what people did on New Year's Eve—they bust guns in the air. But he forgot he was in the suburbs.

They don't play that shit out there. So by the time he got into his car and sped off, the cops were already en route to my house. They caught up with him and attempted to pull him over, but he led them on a seventeen-minute chase that ended with Khalil crashing into a telephone pole. He was immediately charged with resisting arrest and violating his parole. They didn't charge him with murder because he didn't have any guns on him. But they found a gun a couple blocks from where the chase ended, and when they ran tests they found his fingerprints all over it. Ballistics tests proved it was the gun that had wounded me and killed Tina. He was later charged with premeditated murder, one count of attempted third-degree murder, aggravated assault with a deadly weapon, illegal use of a firearm, unlawful possession of a firearm, and the list went on. He was sentenced to life without parole for Tina, an added twenty-five years for what he did to me, and an additional six years for violating his parole and other charges. I was relieved I spent my days surrounded by doctors and nurses and Ms. Carol, my shrink, who all made frequent visits to my house for our sessions. I spent my nights watching reruns of *Sanford and Son*. I couldn't sleep for more than three hours without nightmares reliving the night Tina and I were shot. And when I wasn't having nightmares, I was having migraines.

My doctor prescribed morphine, but I could only get dosages whenever he or my nurse came to my house. He said he didn't feel comfortable leaving that strong a medicine with me until I was more emotionally stable. My life was so different. My living room looked like a hospital room. I had a hospital bed in there and everything, and a doctor or a nurse came by at least four days a week. I opted for house visits because at the time I didn't have anyone to drive me to my doctors' appointments—well, at least that's what I told Ms. Carol. The real reason was that I didn't want to be seen in public with my face wrapped up like some mummy. And even now, after my doctor removed the bandages, I still don't want to be seen. I haven't looked at my face yet, but from what the doctors said about reconstructive surgery, I know it has to be bad. Shit, he was talking about cutting places I didn't even know existed on my face. I've been thinking about it and I really want to get it done because God knows I can't live the rest of my life with a disfigured face. I'd die first. The only thing is, I'm heavily contemplating whether or not I'll go back to living as Celess or give that up, because that decision weighs heavily on what types of surgeries I will get on my face. Ms. Carol said if I decide to live as a woman I might as well let the doctors give me feminine traits while they're reconstructing my face, like go in and raise my eyebrows and stuff. Of course, she said the only way she would allow me to do that was if I planned to get the complete sex change. I either had to be a woman or a man. It was too risky being both. She said she was all for me being happy but not if it would cost me my life, like it almost did.

I swear, I'd only known that lady for a short time but it felt like I'd know her all my life. She was like a mother version of Tina. She treated me like family and always gave me advice, but in a way that a mother would. At first, I wasn't feelin' her. I just knew she was goin' walk her glasses-and-suit-wearin' ass in here and start judgin' me, but she didn't. She actually started our first meeting off with a story about a friend of hers she went to college with, who went through similar situations as me. Not taking it as far as me and Tina, but he was a transvestite and often went back and forth about telling men that he used to be a man himself. He died of brain cancer, though, several years after completing his sex change. One thing had nothing to do with the other, but it was ironic that he was diagnosed with the cancer after all his surgeries. He was only thirty-six. Ms. Carol told me she understood me and could relate to my desire to be a woman. She said her desire to have children was just as strong if not stronger and if she had the opportunity to pretend she had any, she would jump at it, so she understood my taking the opportunity to be a woman. At the same time, though, she let me know that when it came down to hurting other people, that's when it should have stopped. She used herself as an example. She said as bad as she wanted children, she knew it wasn't an option for her to kidnap someone else's. It took me a little while, but I came to respect her point of view. Everything she told me was right. I just wish I didn't have to find out this way. I wish my mom was as capable of communicating with me as Ms. Carol was. Maybe then things would have played out differently for me. But then again, maybe it wasn't all my mom's fault. Maybe I could have been a better listener.

Ring! Ring! Ring!

Hello, you have reached me at a bad time. Please leave a message and I'll call you back at my earliest convenience. God bless. Beep.

"Hello, Mom, it's me, your son," I began.

"It's been a while, I know, but now is the time. Mom, a lot has happened since I last heard your voice, and none of it good. Mom, I can't change who I am and what my sexual preference is, but I can be honest in my appearance. And I wish it wouldn't have taken a tragedy to get me to realize that, but it has. I wish I had been fair and considerate of people's feelings, starting with yours. I'm sorry, Mom. I love you. And despite what I've said in the past, I want to hear from you."

I had taken Tina's advice. I tried to make amends with my mom. Even though she apparently wasn't going to call me back, I felt better. I did my part, and that was all Tina asked. I wasn't bitter about my mom's decision to ignore the message I left on her phone. She would have that to deal with later on down the line. I had too much to concentrate on as it was. I had to worry about reconstructing my life. Besides, God worked in mysterious ways, and people who were without parents were usually brought together, in one way or another, with people who were without children.

Ding-dong! Ding-dong!

"I'm coming," I said as I walked slowly to my front door.

"Somebody has put on some pounds," Ms. Carol said as soon as I opened the door.

I rolled my eyes bashfully and let her into my house. It was a sunny June day. The kind of day I used to say I would die for. The kind of day that Tina and me would have pulled up to a basketball game in a hot car, dressed fly as shit, and preyed on niggas.

"I left the office a little early," Ms. Carol said, smiling, holding a DVD in her hand. "Sit down, I'll put it in. It's *Bringing Down the House*. Hilarious movie. You'll like it," she said as she placed the disc in the DVD player.

I took a seat on the couch. After getting us both a glass of juice and paper plates full of sour cream and onion chips, Ms. Carol joined me. We watched the movie until the credits rolled. Ms. Carol said a few uplifting words and left me with some poetry. Poetry became one of my coping mechanisms. I had even started writing it. I wrote a poem for Tina that I had recited to her at least once every day. I looked at her in the painting of us she gave me for my birthday and read:

I used to wonder why it rained. But flowers have to grow. And why in the winter when trees go bare, flowers have to go.

I learned how to keep myself from missing them, for I knew they'd be back in the spring.

And all summer long I could play in their gardens and embrace all the warmth they would bring.

But then in the fall, I'd prepare my goodbyes as winter was setting in.

And long for the days of spring to return so I could see my flowers again.

Ms. Carol gave me a big hug and I saw her to the door. I went back to my well-worn spot on the couch where I planned to channel-surf until the wee hours of the morning.

There were a lot of bumps in the road to recovery. I had to start over from scratch. I had to find other interests. I had to get used to staying in the house and often alone. I had to release my old ways. I was like a person suddenly losing sight. It was a whole new world for me. I couldn't pick up the phone and call up a guy and have him come over and spend time with me. I couldn't go out to a club and dance and drink and flirt. I couldn't have money thrown at me from different directions. I couldn't take any more flights out to L.A. and wile out with Tina. I was lost. I was through. Just about ready to give up on life.

Ring! Ring!

I answered reluctantly. "Celess?" the voice responded.

"Yes?" I was not believing the voice I heard on the other end of the phone.

"I heard about what happened with you and Tina. I...I haven't been able to stop thinking about you." A tear slid down my cheek before I responded, "Michael, you don't know how good it is to hear your voice."

KINGSTON IMPERIAL

Marvis Johnson — Publisher
Joshua Wirth — Designer
Kristin Clifford — Publicist, Finn Partners
Emilie Moran — Publicist, Finn Partners

Contact:
Kingston Imperial
144 North 7th Street #255
Brooklyn, NY 11249
Email: Info@kingstonimperial.com
www.kingstonimperial.com

I DON'T KNOW WHO NEEDS TO READ THIS BUT...

Overnight Successes Take Years! In 2015 I was trying to make Secret Society into a movie…

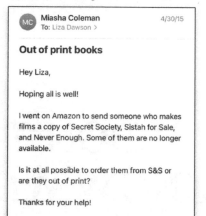

> **MC** **Miasha Coleman** 4/30/15
> To: Liza Dawson >
>
> ### Out of print books
>
> Hey Liza,
>
> Hoping all is well!
>
> I went on Amazon to send someone who makes films a copy of Secret Society, Sistah for Sale, and Never Enough. Some of them are no longer available.
>
> Is it at all possible to order them from S&S or are they out of print?
>
> Thanks for your help!

And again in 2016…

> **MC** **Miasha Coleman** 11/3/16
> To: Liza Dawson >
>
> ### Hey Liza
>
> Hi Liza,
>
> Hope all is well with you and the family!
>
> Recently I had the pleasure of meeting a Producer & President of Tyler Perry Studios.
>
> He asked if I ever thought about turning any of my books into films and of course I said yes. He asked me to get him copies of my books.
>
> My question to you is, does Simon & Schuster have any that can be sent to me to have on hand for situations like this?
>
> Thanks Liza!
>
> Happy upcoming Holidays!

And again in 2017...

MC Miasha Coleman   4/20/17
To: Liza Dawson >

Hey Liza

Hi Liza,

Hoping you and the family are well.

Just wanted to throw something out there to you. I finished up Secret Society the screenplay and so if you come across any opportunities in film that you think would be good for me and my goals please let me know.

My plan is to garner as much support financially, creatively, and production-wise between now and July to hopefully begin shooting in August/September (before the weather gets too cool).

Any leads, advice, etc. will be gladly appreciated.

Best regards,
Miasha

Fast-forward four years and the next email I sent to Liza (poor Liza) about Secret Society the movie was a private link for her to watch it, and this was her response:

Get the Point?! Don't stop, keep pursuing your dreams! When they say no, it just means there's another way. If you come to a dead-end, bust a u-ey. But whatever you do, Do NOT TAKE YOUR FOOT OFF THE GAS!

Ya Girl,

Miasha

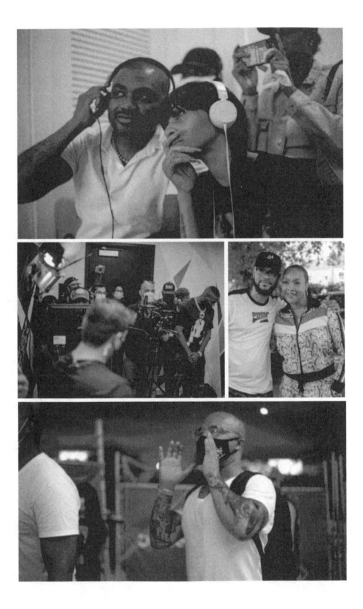

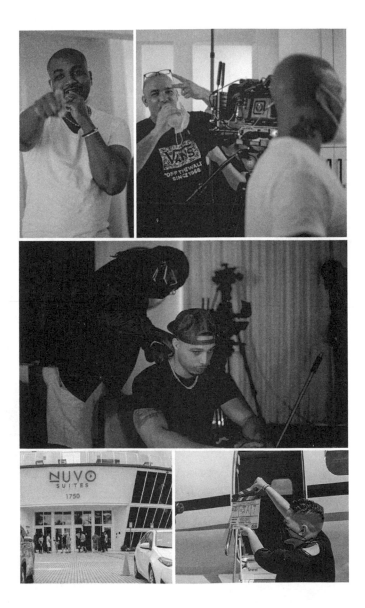

Dear dreamers,

That thing that keeps you up all night and wakes you early in the morning. That thing you've been dreaming of since you were a child, that is called your purpose! When God uniquely designed you he placed something very special inside. This is your calling, go after it with tunnel vision. This journey you are on will be filled with obstacles but I guarantee if you contintue forward starving your distractions and feeding your purpose you'll enjoy the satisfaction of one day saying "I did it!" Ask yourelf, "what kind of legacy will I leave behind for my family?" Now go be great and leave your mark on the world, you are more powerful than you know.

\- Erica Pinkett
"Tina"

No matter how hard it gets you're going to make it. Be consistent, be true to yourself, and live the life you dream of because you only live once. So don't be the same, be better than you were yesterday, your only limit is you!

Reyna♥

\- Reyna Love
"Celess"

WATCH SECRET SOCIETY!

& LET US KNOW WHAT YOU THINK

@SECRETSOCIETYMOVIE
@MIASHAOFFICIAL